BREAD, SALT
AND
Wine

BREAD, SALT AND *Wine*

TARNISHED SOULS

DEV BENTHAM

www.devbentham.com

Tarnished Souls 4: Bread, Salt & Wine

Copyright © June 2013 by Dev Bentham

All rights reserved.

ISBN 978-1-942255-09-3

Original edition editor: Larke Butler

Cover Artist: Jordan Castillo Price

Published by

Love is a Light Press

POB 685, Minocqua, WI 54548

www.devbentham.com

Dedication

for my wonderful friend Marsha,
whose price is above rubies

Acknowledgement

I want to thank Loose Id for originally hosting the Tarnished Souls series. I've had a great time writing these stories. I'm grateful to my wonderful Loose Id editor, Larke Butler, for her insights, graciousness, and humor. For this Love is a Light Press rerelease, Jordan Castillo price designed an amazing new cover. Throughout the writing of this series, she also offered incredible advice and support—she's a Wurlitzer! And because this is the last Tarnished Souls book, it's about time I thanked my amazing rabbi, who I think will be amused to find himself here. As always, I'm grateful to my family and friends (and particularly my sweet husband) for putting up with my tendency to leave my keys in the freezer, the eggs in the cupboard, and all my other absentminded, story-induced fumblings.

Purim is a funny holiday—literally. It's based on the Book of Esther, a biblical story that reads like farce. There's a drunken king, a bevy of virgins, overheard plots, seduction, and plenty of conniving. Purim celebrations involve reading the Book of Esther (the Megillah), dressing in costume, sometimes the staging of a satirical play, and the requirement to drink until you can't distinguish between good and evil. It's just plain fun.

And yet the Purim story deals directly with the potentially deadly consequences of bigotry. All Queen Esther's machinations are designed to thwart the evil Haman, who is intent on destroying the Jews. Likewise in this story,

Kenny's playfulness constitutes a direct battle with the forces of homophobia. Hamans come in many guises, sometimes appearing as members of our own families and wreaking havoc on our psyches. In this way George has been wounded by hatred. Only love, hard work, and learning to hold himself more lightly can save him. L'chaim.

LOS ANGELES

2005: An April Wedding

The band was too loud, the bride looked like a skeleton, and I had a raging headache. What a way to spend Friday night. I kept trying to remember why working for a prestigious LA restaurant had seemed like a better deal than my comfortable line job at a respectable place in New York. Especially since this particular gig had required supervising the creation of hundreds of puffy cheese minisoufflés, artichoke and bacon rolls, and duck liver wraps, all of which had to be carted from the L'Ouest kitchens to this golf-course-sized Beverley Hills backyard, where a chubby record company executive was marrying Madam Skeletor in lavish style.

It wasn't the menu I would have suggested for this fat-conscious crowd, but until I could convince my boss to offer less pretentious and difficult-to-serve food, I'd be stuck with whatever he arranged. And unpretentious wasn't of particular value to Stephan—that's pronounced "Stefaaan"—Becker.

Any sane chef would design a separate menu for catering, featuring finger food, fresh fruits, and meals that could be plated with grace. I looked at the tiny bites of rich food starting to congeal in the warming trays and considered whether it was time to bring a new batch from the van.

A silver platter appeared at my left elbow, and a voice suggested, "I can start offering those to the guests so you can freshen up this station."

I turned, and there he was. A few inches shorter than me, with spiky blond hair and a big smile, he wore the standard waiter's uniform of black pants and a black button-down shirt. He managed to look like he'd just stepped off the runway during New York's fashion week.

He held out the tray. "You're Mr. Zajac, the new catering chef, right? I'm Kenny Marks, waiter extraordinaire." He had an exuberant lilt to his voice. "And I'd love to help you get rid of that food."

I could use a friend on staff. "Call me George. You seem to know your way around. Have you worked for L'Ouest long?"

He held the platter while I arranged the food. "I was with the company for the first event, a horrid little birthday party." He shuddered dramatically. "The wife had decorated the whole house in black for the poor man's fortieth. It was brutal."

"This is my first job catering." I nodded toward the crowd. "Any advice you have for me would be appreciated."

Kenny looked out at the gathering. "You see that guy in the maroon bow tie? He's the groom's financial manager. Make sure he's happy. That's where your check and your tip are coming from. And over there's the bride's mother. Rumor is that back home in Dallas she hosts soirees on a regular basis. She and the daughter are supposed to be close. You might give the mama some personal attention—people like to meet the chef, makes them feel special. The new couple is bound to entertain, and I doubt our blushing bride cooks. She'll ask mummy for advice on catering. Tips are always bigger from repeat customers."

I stared at him. "How do you know all this?"

He hefted the now full platter to his shoulder. "I keep my eyes and ears open. Here comes Libby Spencer. She's the most sought-after wedding planner in the city. Be very, very nice to her."

With that he strolled off, walking with shoulders back and a slight sway to his hips, his pants pleasingly tight across a very nice ass. What would it be like to feel that comfortable with one's sexuality? The question made me break into a sweat.

I turned my attention to Ms. Spencer. Striding toward me, tall, thin, with four-inch spiked heels that clicked on the stone pavement, she looked as formidable as any corporate attorney I'd known back in the day.

I smiled and stepped forward.

She thrust out her hand. "Libby Spencer. Call me Libby. You're the new catering chef. George, is it? I hope you're better than the little weasel L'Ouest had before. For some reason my customers like to hire your company. Mostly for the name, I think. This"—she gestured at the food—"wouldn't be my first choice of event food, but c'est la vie."

I nodded. "Perhaps we could adjust the menu."

She snorted. "Not likely, not with your prig of a chef. Never mind. You'll find I'm easy to work with as long as things go smoothly."

From a distance, I could see Skeletor gesturing toward us. Libby plastered on a brilliant smile. Out of the corner of her mouth she muttered, "This job has plenty of headaches. Don't be one of them." With that, she was gone.

I signaled one of the other waiters to replenish the warming trays. When I had everything looking good, I left an assistant in charge of the buffet and went in search of the mother of the bride. It wouldn't hurt to spread a little charm.

Kenny beamed at me from across the room. He really had a great smile.

* * * *

It was after midnight by the time we got everything cleaned up and stowed away back at the restaurant. I got change for the five one-hundred-dollar bills the financial manager had pressed into my palm as we left, and doled out fifty dollars to each of the four waiters, the busboy/

dishwasher, and the bartender. I stuffed one into my pocket and the others into an envelope to give the kitchen crew.

The group started toward the staff locker room, and the kitchen emptied out. Except the cute one, Kenny.

He waved his money at me. "And the momma? Was she pleased?"

I shrugged. "She says she'll call if she needs catering. We'll see." He watched me expectantly until I added, "Thanks for pointing her out."

"No problem. Glad to be of service." He shifted his weight onto one hip and looked at me from under his eyelashes. "Chef sometimes forgets to schedule me. Maybe you could put in a good word."

I nodded. He smiled and turned to leave, throwing a "good night" over his shoulder as he sauntered out the door. I stayed behind to check on the preparations for the next event, Sunday brunch for a hundred. I reviewed the work schedule and was surprised by the pang of disappointment I felt when Kenny Marks's name wasn't on the list.

By the time I made it back to the staff locker room, everyone was gone. I tossed my white coat and hat into the laundry bin and gathered my jacket and helmet. Outside, my motorcycle started immediately, and I pulled out into the warm California night.

The breeze was cool, and the thrum of the engine under my thighs gave me a feeling of power and grace. Traffic was light, and my tiredness started to melt as I sped through quiet streets. There were places I could go where people would be awake. Hot rooms with loud music and willing men. For a few minutes I let myself imagine entering the bar, scanning the crowd, and finding someone who was looking back at me with the same hunger. I shook my head. My jaw still hurt from the last overzealous cowboy I'd let ride my face. What I needed was something safer, more predictable. Not a boyfriend. I wouldn't inflict myself on anyone. But maybe I could find a regular fuck buddy who could deal with my sexual weirdness without getting too rough.

By the time I pulled into the garage, the desire for company had passed. I parked the bike and climbed the stairs to my apartment. In New York I never lived lower than the sixth floor. In Echo Park none of the apartments in my price range sat higher than the third.

The apartment building was quiet, with only the distant sounds of traffic and the pound of a rap song from somewhere down the street. I opened the door and stepped into my tiny haven. One of the many reasons I should never have married Anne was the mismatch in our living styles. Where she favored cozy contemporary, my preferred decor was stripped-down minimalism. She called it empty. I liked to think of it as sparse, monastic, Zen. For years we compromised. She decorated the apartment. I lived at the office. It was only after I moved out that I realized how hard it had been for me to breath surrounded by all that stuff. Okay, maybe decor wasn't the only reason I'd felt stifled.

I'd liked the simplicity of the second-floor studio the first time I saw it. Essentially one large room, it had a rudimentary kitchen along one wall, and windows and the doorway to the balcony along another. I'd furnished it with a big bed, a low bureau, and plenty of space. The only other furniture was the wrought-iron table and two chairs that filled the small balcony. I crossed to the kitchen and poured myself a glass of Australian chardonnay, crisp with vanilla and apple notes, and at less than ten bucks a bottle, an unsung bargain. I slid open the balcony door and sat to watch the city sleep.

I grew up miserable in the middle of cornfields. I'd felt so fucking isolated. I vowed that as soon as I could escape, I'd live in places where there'd always be someone who could hear me if I screamed. It soothed me to watch people and cars moving along crowded streets. I sipped my wine and relished watching the lights of cars. It had taken a long time for me to get there, safe, single, and unknown. So what if I was lonely? Everything had its price.

* * * *

I fell asleep thinking of the way Kenny's pants hugged the curve of his ass.

And woke shaking from a dream so real I could hear the animals breathing, smell the warm mix of hay and cow combined with a pungent tang of fresh manure. I lay staring into the darkness, listening to the pound of my heart and the memory of my father's voice, alternating between whispering love and shouting the condemnation of God and all his angels.

"Pray, boy."

I was twelve again, naked and shamed, fighting not to cry as my father's belt bit into my flesh and his words seared themselves into my heart.

"Pray."

I slid from the bed onto my knees and pressed my hands together hard, imitating prayer to a God I no longer believed in, holding the position until my knees ached and the muscles in my shoulders burned. It was the only way to make the dream recede. If there was a God, he wasn't fooled by my fakery, but my subconscious was, and eventually I crawled back in bed and drifted toward sleep.

My father couldn't whip my abomination away, but some wounds never heal, and it was folly for me to believe I'd ever be fit for anything other than a quick, hard fuck in a dark alley.

* * * *

I woke early, still edgy from my dream. Sun streaked in the studio window, making the floors shine. I was a sporadic exerciser at best. Back in New York I would have taken the elevator down to the basement to work out in a dark room that smelled like gym socks. In Southern California I didn't need a treadmill. I could walk along palm-tree-lined streets listening to birdsong. I rolled out of bed into old sweats and running shoes and shoved a wad of bills in my pocket.

Outside a breeze smelled of exhaust and piss. Trash blew along the curb. I started to walk quickly, plotting a path that would bring me near a bakery I'd spotted a few days before. Instead of palm-tree-lined streets, I found myself striding beside gray buildings covered with graffiti, past a drive-through dry cleaner and a mesh-fronted liquor store. I turned a corner. Ahead of me the street passed under the freeway. As I neared, I could see movement in the undergrowth behind the fence. Dozens of people moved around, rolled up bedding, chatted, and stuffed their belongings into packs, plastic bags, and shopping carts. I looked away and walked under the overpass.

I was used to seeing homeless people. The last place I lived was New York City, for God's sake. But something about watching the hillside come alive like that shook me. I kept walking until I found the bakery I'd been meaning to try. Sweet things comforted me. One of my earliest memories was of my mom handing me a cookie warm from the oven while my ass still stung from my dad's belt. No wonder I was fucked up.

The bakery smelled of yeast and caramelized sugar. I ordered coffee and a dozen doughnuts to go. On a bench outside the bakery, I sat drinking coffee and basking in the spring sun.

In front of me, a woman climbed out of a battered green sedan. She stretched and yawned before opening the back door. I saw her shake sleeping children awake. One, two, three, they piled out of the car and stood blinking beside her in pajamas, with their hair mussed and sleep lines creasing their faces. The woman shouldered a giant, brightly colored cloth bag, slung her youngest onto her hip, held the middle girl's hand, looked both ways, and crossed the street. The oldest, a boy of maybe seven, skipped ahead. I watched as they all entered a gas station. I ate a doughnut and licked the sweet stickiness from my fingers. As I pulled another from the bag, the little family emerged, looking freshly washed and neatly dressed. They crossed the street, headed for the car. The girl—who couldn't have been more than five—spotted me, or rather, my doughnut. After maybe twenty gawking seconds, she looked down at her shoes. The mom considered me. I guess I looked safe enough, because she simply nodded and opened the car door so the kids could pile in.

I looked from my bag of doughnuts and to the car full of undoubtedly hungry kids. Not that doughnuts were a nutritious breakfast. But they tasted good—soft, cakey with a hint of cinnamon. She was closing her door by the time I got there. I knocked on the window. She looked up at me with quick suspicion.

"Sorry. Didn't mean to startle you. I thought the kids might like some doughnuts." I held up the bag.

Her eyes narrowed.

I patted my belly. "If I eat any more of these, the exercise I got this morning isn't going to make any difference." She kept staring at me. I could hear rustling in the backseat, but I held her gaze and put on my best Iowa farm-boy smile. "No hidden agenda, ma'am. Just thought your kids could use these more than me." I set the bag on the roof of the car and walked away.

By the time I walked back under the overpass, the crowd of folks sleeping along the highway had scattered. A couple of men sat on the curb talking. A few more stood by the on-ramp with signs advertising that they'd work for food. An old woman shouted curses as she pushed an overflowing shopping cart along the road. I thought about sweetness. I might have had ghosts and demons banging around in my head, but at least I had a home, a job, and hope.

And I didn't need to be at work until the next morning, and I knew how to make doughnuts. When I got home, I looked up the nearest restaurant supply company, hopped on my bike, and drove off in search of a deep fat fryer. Maybe I couldn't change the world, but I might be able to make a few people's lives a little sweeter.

* * * *

Less than a week passed before, as Kenny had predicted, Bride Skeletor's mother called to arrange a meeting about catering her daughter's first cocktail party. Although the party was months away and the happy couple was still on holiday, Mom was eager to make the arrangements as soon as possible. As I scheduled a consultation with her, I was amazed. I'd thought it would be ages before I had an opportunity to organize something on my own.

Chef Stephan was yelling at a young prep cook when I set down the phone. He was a small, precise man with a sharp tongue honed over thirty years in high-powered kitchens, and his style was to keep order by beating the staff into compliance. If I had been running my own kitchen, I wouldn't have chosen his particular mix of venom and haughty distance, but I'd only been in the business a few years, so what did I know?

As soon as I had him alone, I got to the point. "I'd like to develop a few dishes especially for the catering menu."

His face hardened. "What's wrong with what we offer?"

I used my calm-the-client voice, developed through years of reassuring nervous investors who had trusted me with their life savings. "Wouldn't it be better to have a few offerings suited to both our working conditions and to lighter palates?"

"No." He stood with his hands on his hips and scowled like a bulldog. "The menu will not change."

In my old life, before I became a cook, I spent a lot of time with people who were used to getting their way. I had been one of them.

I inclined my head in deference to his oh-so-muchness and asked, "Why not?"

His arm exploded out from his body as he made a sweeping gesture that encompassed the kitchen, the dining room, and the universe beyond. "Because when people contact us for catering, they expect the L'Ouest menu. They are asking to bring the restaurant into their living room. And that is what we give them."

I shook my head. "I doubt they are looking to re-create exact meals they've had here. I think they're expecting excellent food with a French twist."

"You're wrong." He waved his hand to dismiss me.

I wanted to ask, If you don't want my input, why the fuck did you hire me? I bit my tongue and left.

* * * *

"Heard you stood up to the devil the other day." Kenny was helping me set out the artichoke salads it had taken the kitchen crew hours to plate and which would take the corporate meeting goers we were serving minutes to eat.

"If you mean Chef, it didn't do any good." I watched Kenny's hands as he placed the plates on the table. He had a knack for lining up the artichoke in perfect alignment with the knife every time. He had great hands, with elegant fingers, the masculine brush of hair at the base of each hand in sexy contrast to his manicured fingernails. I shook my head. Fantasizing about a coworker. Maybe I needed to visit the bars again after all.

Kenny was speaking. "I should have warned you. He's fanatic about the menu. If he weren't such a homophobic little twit, I'd think he had a hard-on for Louis XIV."

"He's homophobic?" I kept my voice level, trying not to betray the creep of fear Kenny's statement had triggered.

"A real prick about it. Rumor is he fired two guys for making out in the alley during break." Kenny kept talking as he placed the salads in perfect rows. "Check the schedule. Anyone he thinks is gay gets fewer shifts."

I scowled at him. The whole subject made me profoundly uncomfortable.

Kenny shrugged. "Sorry. Didn't mean to offend."

The door opened, and executives in crisp suits began filing in. From the smiles and laughter, I surmised that whatever the meeting was about, it signaled a waterfall of money. By the time I turned to Kenny to apologize for being so abrupt, he was gone. Tray in hand, he was sauntering through the crowd, handing out champagne.

I left him to it and went back to our rented kitchen to check on the entrées. I'd been on the job for less than a month, and I already knew to be relieved when the job included the use of kitchen facilities on-site. Granted, the word kitchen appeared to mean different things in different places, but anything beat having to prep everything back at the restaurant in the early morning, before the regular kitchen staff arrived. Or worse yet, having to work around them and risk the wrath of Chef Stephan.

Cheryl, my best line chef—a short, thin woman with wild red curls—smiled as I entered the spacious kitchen in the building basement. "Hey, boss, ready for the soup yet?"

I glanced at the soup bowls lined up along the stainless steel counter like overturned porcelain hats. "Not yet. I'll page you when the first salad plate empties. We should be able to get all four carts in the service elevator, but if you need to take a second trip—"

"We'll be fine. Relax. We've done this before."

"Sorry." Corporate events made me jumpy. It was too strange to be on the other side of the serving table.

"Everything's going smoothly." She made a shooing gesture, sweeping me out of the kitchen. "Don't worry about us."

As I took the service elevator back to the top floor, I wondered why Cheryl didn't have my job. She had more experience, knew the city and the clients. Did the company have a policy of not hiring from within? I needed to get around to reading the employee handbook.

As the elevator door opened I saw Kenny and another waiter standing by the door, each carrying a large tray of dirty glassware.

"I don't even know if he's—" Kenny broke off as the door opened. His eyes widened when he saw me. He blushed. Kitchens can be capricious places. Maybe the last catering chef had discouraged talk among the waiters. I gave them both a nod and a smile and held the door open to show that it was fine with me. As long as the guests didn't hear, what did I care what they talked about? Kenny was a good waiter. I made a mental note to have him on crew as often as possible.

* * * *

"The swishy writer?" Chef Stephan scowled at me over the soup stock he was tasting.

I winced. Kenny didn't miss much, did he? "He's one of the best I've worked with, efficient and courteous. The customers like him."

Chef shrugged. "To each his own. He gives me the creeps, but if you want him on your team permanently, I don't care. It's your stomach."

I gritted my teeth. "Thank you, Chef."

At least he was letting me have a say in my crew. I went back to my desk to get ready for my consultation with Skeletor's mom, wondering if her daughter's kitchen was big enough. Preparing our signature heavy hors d'oeuvres would be more pleasant and practical away from Chef Stephan's toxic kitchen.

2005: A July Wedding

It was Saturday night, and I was standing behind the buffet, wasting my acclaimed knife skills carving individual portions of roast suckling pig. We'd finished most of the serving and were waiting on a few folks hungry for seconds. With any luck the happy couple would cut the cake soon, and we'd be free to clean up the main course.

Out on the floor I watched Kenny gracefully scoop up a dirty plate and balance it on his tray. I liked the way he did that, smooth, like a dancer. A regular guy wouldn't look like that. He'd be too afraid of what other people might say. Yeah, right, regular. A regular guy like me, whose father beat the swish out of him.

The best man stood up and launched into one of those raunchy toasts that sound funny at the time, when everyone has had too much champagne, and end up cringe-worthy on the video.

As everyone clapped and held up their glasses, Kenny slid behind me and whispered, "I think maybe I should lighten up on his champagne."

I shook my head. "Too late. Better let him enjoy the night—he'll be embarrassed enough tomorrow."

A bridesmaid gave a more subdued and sober toast. The father of the bride was succinct, if slurred, and that was that.

As the bride and groom posed around a five-tiered cake, I signaled my crew to start quietly hauling food back to the kitchen. More of a staging space than a kitchen, at least it was far enough away from the main hall that we could clean up in peace.

Kenny appeared with a tray of dirty plates and glasses. He shivered extravagantly and gestured toward the pig. "Wouldn't my granny roll over in her grave to see me so close to that vile piece of traif."

I raised an eyebrow.

"Unclean, not kosher." He waved his hand dismissively. "Don't worry. I'm not very religious. More of what you might call a holiday Jew. And"—he paused dramatically—"I've been with my share of pigs."

I laughed. "Like the best man?"

He smiled at me. "What a guy, eh? Did you notice the groom wasn't laughing?"

I shrugged, concentrating on slicing up pig to send home with the family. "Aren't they all like that? At my wedding the best man was so busy hitting on the bridesmaids he could barely be bothered to toast us."

There was a silence. I looked up from the pig to see Kenny's face in a funny half smile. "You were married?"

"Ten years."

"What happened?"

I looked around the kitchen. Cheryl, two prep cooks, and another waiter were busy with their own tasks, but I could feel them listening. I mumbled, "Didn't take."

He set his tray down and picked up an empty one. He turned toward the door, saying, "Funny, I didn't figure you for the marrying type."

A familiar shame washed over me. I ought to have been brave enough to tell the truth about myself. But every time I considered it, my heart raced, and the memory of cow shit, humiliation, and hay filled my nose. For all his affectations, Kenny was twice the man I was. I envied his bravery but wasn't about to follow his example.

I turned back to the pig carcass.

* * * *

Skeletor's kitchen turned out to be a huge room with commercial-grade appliances and acres of counter space. I had the crew meet me there and arranged for Kenny to come in early to help plate. He might not have been the most logical choice as a helper—after all, he was a waiter, not a cook—but I figured he needed the hours. If Cheryl found it odd, she didn't comment.

"It's my oldest daughter," Cheryl was saying. "She's driving me crazy. Twenty-one and she thinks she knows it all."

Kenny gave her a sympathetic smile. "Didn't we all at that age?"

I nodded. At twenty-one I was caught in a fight between fantasies about my college roommate and nightmares about my father and the barn. When the nightmares won, I married Anne.

Cheryl gestured toward Kenny with her knife. "Last night she told me she's having an affair with a married man. A married man. It breaks my heart."

Kenny shuddered. "I don't think I could do that. I mean, I know people who have, I'm not saying I'm better than them, but I'd get too weirded out thinking about the wife and maybe kids."

Cheryl closed her eyes. When she opened them, she went back to slicing beef into thin strips for the roll-ups. "The thing that makes it worse is that she knows her daddy cheated on me. I don't get what she's thinking."

I finished another duck roll and handed it to Kenny to put on the tray. "She's probably not thinking. She's going with her gut."

After a moment's silence, Cheryl asked, "How did your marriage end?"

I looked up. It was only the three of us in the kitchen. "It never should have begun. But we were young and stupid. I wasn't attentive enough, and she got swept off her feet by my business partner. Ex-business partner now."

"Where is she?" Kenny asked, his eyes on the tray.

I shrugged. "Still in New York. They live in our old apartment near the park."

"Ouch." Cheryl winced.

"Yeah. I don't blame her. I wasn't much of a husband." All those years of wanting something I thought I couldn't have and settling for something I had to work hard to want. It still made my bile rise to think of all those wasted years.

I shook my head. "Enough about me. What are you going to tell your daughter?"

* * * *

A few days later we were halfway through setting up for a barbecue in the backyard of one of those movie-mogul mansions in Beverly Hills.

"Shit." I looked at the trays of food stacked on a cart next to the folding tables. "We forgot the linens. And dessert—where's dessert? I'm going to have to go back."

Two of my waiters stared at me. Kenny bounced on his toes. "Need help?"

I looked at him. It wouldn't take two of us, but on the other hand, there wasn't much for the three of them to do while I was gone, and I could use the company.

"Sure." I gestured toward the bar. "In the meantime, you two get that set up."

Kenny followed me to the van, keeping up a stream of pleasant, if not very consequential banter. It was still early. With any luck we'd make it to the restaurant and back before the clients showed up and wondered what was happening.

"You want me to drive?" Kenny asked as we neared the van. "I know a few shortcuts."

I tossed him the keys. "I'm lucky when I can get to work without getting lost."

He laughed. "I remember. It took me a long time to learn my way around."

I swung up into the seat beside him. "It's all the freeways that get me. I make one wrong turn, and I'm funneled miles out of my way."

Kenny adjusted the seat and the mirror before starting the van. He looked over his left shoulder for a long moment and pulled out. "I've seen you coming in on your motorcycle, all butch and manly."

I laughed. "It's a piece-of-shit Yamaha—hardly a bad-boy bike. Gets good gas mileage, though." I settled back in the seat as Kenny took a left. This wasn't the way we came, but if he knew better, that was great. "I miss subways. In New York I never drove."

"Why'd you move?"

I shrugged. "My past life kept catching up with me. I was ready for a change."

He grinned. "In the witness protection program, are you? I can see you working for the mafia in New York. They'd call you the Blond Menace, the Plains Killer." He looked over. "Although, to tell the truth, if I was casting you for a movie, I'd pick you as California born and bred. You've got that wholesome beach-boy look."

I snorted. "Stephan told me you were a writer. Casting me in a movie would take some imagination."

He glanced at me. "I don't know about that. Tall, square jaw, blue eyes—you look like leading-man material to me."

I frowned. "I'm too old and fat to be a lead."

His let his gaze graze over me before going back to the road. "You're not old. You're what, thirty-five? And I think a man looks good with a little meat on his bones."

The air felt thick in the van. I cleared my throat. "Thirty-eight. And, um, thanks. So what do you write?"

Kenny visibly straightened. "I was a novelist. These days I'm trying my hand at screenwriting. After all, when in Rome and all that. Literature's dead. The screen is where it's at. Have you always been a chef?"

I shook my head. "Hell no. Until three years ago I'd never been in a commercial kitchen."

"Ah, the past life when you were a hit man."

"Nothing that glamorous. Investment banker."

Kenny crowed, "I knew it. I knew you were a crook." He wrinkled his nose. "Oops, did I go too far?"

"No, you're right. The whole system is corrupt."

"I can see it now. A man of integrity, you were sucked into the dark world of high finance and…"

"I thought you'd decided I was a crook."

He nodded vigorously. "Exactly. An ethical criminal. Don't you love the complexity?"

I held up my hands to stop him. "Hold up, Oscar Wilde. I'm not one of your characters."

He beamed at me. "That's the nicest thing anyone's said to me all day."

"That I'm not one of your characters?"

"No, silly, you called me Oscar Wilde. That's lovely. Thank you."

"Um, you're welcome."

"So why did you leave banking if it wasn't your integrity or to enter the witness protection program?"

I watched the houses as we drove down a backstreet. "Do you know where you're going?"

"Absolutely. And don't be evasive." He shrugged. "I mean, unless you want to be."

I closed my eyes and pictured myself at my big desk in my bright office. "On my thirty-fifth birthday I went to work in the morning, and by the afternoon I'd decided my whole life was a fraud. I quit my job and went home to leave my wife."

"Wow. Happy fucking birthday."

"Should have done it years before."

I stared out the window, not wanting to see the compassion in his eyes.

We rode in silence until there it was before us, the restaurant, appearing from this angle like a mirage. Kenny pulled into the parking lot, and the moment was broken.

* * * *

It was nine in the morning, and I had the whole crew down at the restaurant loading the van. We were due at a ranch thirty miles from town for a two o'clock reception. What with traffic and setup, my goal was to get us on the road by ten. If it were my company, I would have equipped the van with warming ovens and refrigerators to make the process easier. As it was, we'd need to get there early, commandeer the ranch oven, and station a cook to rotate the food through. It continued to drive me crazy that Chef Stephan refused to even talk about modifying the catering menu to accommodate reality.

Today we'd be helping a software executive celebrate his fortieth birthday, a task that would require our entire crew, hundreds of pounds of food, and enough alcohol to inebriate a small army. I was already in a foul mood. My own fortieth birthday was only a few years away, and I was living like a student in a small apartment, no closer to resolving my issues, no one steady in my life, not even a regular fuck, and my only real friends lived somewhere else. While I had some New York–earned money in the bank, my life seemed as cold as the shrimp cocktail I was packing in ice.

It didn't help when I walked outside and heard Kenny whining to Cheryl, "It's crazy. I've never fallen for a straight guy before."

Kenny's love life was none of my business, so I cleared my throat to let them know I was there. He blushed and stammered something about getting the next load before sliding through the door past me.

It made me livid to think that Kenny was involved with some straight guy who was probably fulfilling a fantasy and would drop him when he got tired. Kenny deserved so much more. It took serious courage to be as out, as fucking flamboyant as Kenny was. And the guy was smart. And funny. And a damned good writer. I'd looked him up online and been impressed. Just the thought of some straight guy running his hands through Kenny's spiky hair or seeing him shirtless—having access to that strong, supple body and those oh so mobile lips—it made me furious.

I barked an order at Cheryl. She looked startled.

"Sorry," I mumbled. "Didn't mean to sound so sharp. Let's load this stuff and get out of here."

She gave me an odd look and walked back into the kitchen. I took a deep breath. I didn't need to take my bad temper out on the crew. It was none of my business what Kenny did outside company time.

We crammed the van full. I let Cheryl take the wheel, still not confident driving around the city. Four waiters, the bartender, and two kitchen helpers piled into a couple cars to caravan out to the ranch.

Cheryl navigated onto the freeway, where traffic was Saturday-morning light. The sky was a clear California blue. Kids would be going to the beach, regular people would be sleeping in, and here we were heading into the hills to cater to some stupid aging executive who was probably living a lie anyway.

"You want to talk about it?" Cheryl asked.

I wrenched my gaze away from the miles of concrete I'd been contemplating. "Talk about what?"

She gave me a look. "Whatever it is that's got your panties in a twist this morning."

I frowned. "I'm fine. I wish Stephan would let me modify the fucking van."

"Uh-huh," she murmured. "Is that it?"

I nodded and looked out the window. Eventually I asked, "So what's the story with this straight guy Kenny's seeing?"

She turned and stared at me for a moment. Returning her focus to the road, she said, "I don't think they're involved. It's more of a crush thing."

That was a relief. At least Kenny wasn't wasting himself on some unappreciative asshole. "That's good."

We were silent for a while.

Cheryl asked, "How about you? Are you seeing anyone?"

"Me?" I shook my head. "Nah."

"Why not?"

I shrugged. "Since I moved here I haven't had time for anything serious. You?"

She laughed. "I have two children still in high school. The last thing I need is someone else to take care of." She paused. "And the question wasn't an invitation."

"I didn't think it was." I looked at her. She was a beautiful woman in my general age group and one of the closest things I had to a friend in LA. I didn't want to hurt her feelings. I stepped hard on my panic. I could do this, could get honest with one person. I cleared my throat. "Um, Cheryl, you're... If I was... I'm gay."

She gaped at me.

"Car," I shouted, pointing to the sedan slowing ahead of us. I had a fleeting thought that we were about to prove my father right that the wages of sin were death.

Cheryl hit the brakes. The van slowed jerkily. We suffered the loss of a few canapés but nothing else.

"You okay?" I asked.

"Fine." She kept her eyes on the road. "You startled me. I thought you were married. Like to a woman. We all did."

"I come from a very religious family. I was twenty-one when I married Anne. By the time I decided I didn't care if I went to hell for being gay, we were already there." I took a deep breath. "I'd rather you didn't spread it around."

She frowned at me. "You don't want me to tell anyone you're gay?"

"I'd rather you didn't."

"Not anyone?" At my look, she shook her head. "Life's complicated, isn't it?"

I nodded. It sure was.

2005: A September Wedding

"What's the point of hiring a historic theater for your wedding and lighting it in pink neon?"

Libby, the wedding coordinator, and I were standing in the aisle of the most recent hot venue. I'd catered three weddings in the space in as many months, but this was the first one that had turned the venerable old opera house—with its gilded paneling and elaborate tile floor—into a little girl's dollhouse.

Beside me, Libby shook her head. "Don't blame me. I just follow orders. It's going to be tricky. She wants to get married up there on the stage with the guests sitting in rows on the dais. Then drinks on the roof and dinner back down here in the theater. Which gives you less than an hour to flip the space. Can you do it?"

I surveyed the theater, imagining my waiters moving chairs and tables. "If I bring in extra staff. Can we use the same chairs?"

She made a note in her ever-present leather-bound notebook. "That'd be the easiest. I'll arrange for the tables and chairs. You bring the linens." She tapped her pencil against her lips, her gaze fixed on the space. "The head count is three-fifty and climbing."

I stared at her. "Climbing? But the wedding is two weeks away."

Libby arched an eyebrow at me. "That's not the least of it. When she hired me eighteen months ago, the groom's name was Pete. Now it's Brian."

"He changed his name?"

"More like she changed horses in the middle of the stream." At my openmouthed expression, she laughed. "It's Hollywood. You know what they say. The show must go on."

I was still shaking my head as we turned to go.

Libby muttered, "You wouldn't believe how many phone calls I had to make to get that damned name changed on everything from the napkins to the honeymoon reservations." She sighed. "It pays my rent, but some days I wish they'd all elope."

* * * *

I told myself I kept scheduling Kenny for extra hours in the kitchen because he was a good worker and needed the money. Truth was, I liked having him around. The kitchen seemed a brighter place whenever he was in it. Cheryl and I were prepping roulades de boeuf—beef rolls stuffed with pork, garlic, and thyme—for an electronics company awards banquet. Two prep cooks worked on salads, and Kenny played gofer and kept us entertained.

"I think the most embarrassing was when I walked in on the bride blowing the best man."

"No." Cheryl stopped sautéing onions to stare at him. "You did not."

He gave an elaborate, vaudevillian shrug. "What can I say? Someone dropped a bottle of wine. I ran back to the utility closet to get a mop, opened the door, and there she was, on her knees, deep throating the best man." One of the prep cooks giggled, and he winked at her. "I offered to take her place, but they declined."

Cheryl laughed. "Now I know that's a lie."

I concentrated on centering a glob of filling on the meat before rolling it up. I had a sudden image of Kenny's mouth encircling a penis. Blinking, I brought my attention back to what I was doing, but looking at the thick, round cylinder of beef didn't help.

The giggling prep cook spoke. "If I was going to cheat on the day of my wedding, that's not how I'd do it."

"In the closet?" Cheryl's eyes slid toward me.

"No." She shuddered. "I mean with a blowjob. I don't get the appeal. I mean, of giving them. Obviously guys like them, but…ew."

The other prep cook, a young man with bad skin and a penchant for tie-dyed head scarves, frowned. "I feel sorry for your boyfriend."

She shrugged. "He gets one on his birthday. That's enough."

Kenny smiled at her. "Maybe it's his fault you don't like them."

Cheryl piped in. "Hygiene can be so important."

The two prep cooks spoke at the same time.

"Ew. I mean, really ew."

"That's nasty, man."

Kenny gave a sage nod. "Hygiene, good point. How about head holding? I hate it when they hold my head."

Cheryl and the blushing woman prep cook murmured their agreement.

"I don't know." It came out before I could stop myself. Probably because I was staring at a thick beef roll, remembering the last time I'd asked someone to shove his cock down my throat.

The kitchen went dead silent. I looked up. Cheryl was stifling a laugh, and the two prep cooks gawked.

A slow smile spread across Kenny's face. "To each his own. Right, boss?"

Fuck. My heart rate doubled, and I looked around for the exit. A moment passed. Nothing bad happened. I took a deep breath and considered the kitchen crew, who had all gone back to work. Gradually my panic drained. Kenny was watching me, concern in his eyes. I shook my head and tried to get back on task, rolling cylinders of cold, flaccid beef.

* * * *

We got the food loaded into the van with an hour to spare. I sent the cooks home and told Kenny to be back in an hour.

"What are you going to do in the meantime?" he asked.

I looked around the clean kitchen. I was caught up on paperwork, and the phone calls I needed to make could wait until the next day. "I don't know. Maybe fix something to eat. There won't be time for dinner once we start work."

He leaned against a counter. "Want some company?"

I blinked. Why not? "Sure. The regular restaurant crew will be here in a few minutes, so why don't we retreat to my office."

He leaped forward. "Sounds like a plan. What can I do?"

When we were settled in my office with reheated portions of the previous day's special in our laps, I raised my water glass to him. "It would be better with Cabernet, but this will have to do."

"Cheers."

We ate for a few minutes in silence. The tiny room felt even smaller with him in it. Outside we could hear the sounds of people arriving at work, chatting, opening and closing lockers. And then the sounds grew more distant as the crew migrated toward the kitchen. Chef Stephan's voice barked orders, and I was glad we'd closed the door.

We were almost through when Kenny cleared his throat. He stared down at his plate and said, "Some friends of mine opened a play last weekend. It's experimental theater. They comped me two tickets for Wednesday night." He looked up. "There's nothing on the calendar that night. Do you want to go? With me?"

My pulse raced. "Are you asking me out on a date?"

"That would be my first choice. But I'm flexible." He grinned. "Very flexible, actually."

I looked into his warm brown eyes and felt the world shifting beneath me. Objections rose like corks in my mind. I was his boss. We worked together. He was too gay, and I was too fucked up. The office felt even smaller. A fluttery feeling in my stomach made it hard to breathe. I looked at Kenny, at his spiked blond hair and the way it contrasted with his dark eyebrows and deep brown eyes. At the five o'clock shadow he'd need to shave before we went to our next event. At his broad shoulders, the way his torso tapered, and the strong thighs filling his jeans.

Kenny puffed his cheeks and blew out a big gust of air. "Right. No big deal. I thought you might want to—"

"Sure." The word came out without me consciously thinking it.

Kenny's whole face brightened. "Really, you'll come? That's great. Really great."

I nodded. "Right. In the meantime we should—"

"Yeah, it's about time to get ready." He jumped up. "I'll take your plate."

As his hand brushed mine I felt a jolt of excitement. I blinked up at him. Kenny bit his lower lip, held my gaze for a moment longer, and then he was gone.

I sat staring after him, fear and arousal churning lunch around my stomach. Was I making a mistake? Probably. And yet the promise in that touch... I shook my head. We had a dinner to serve.

* * * *

We were ten minutes into the set change in the old theater when I heard Libby gasp. She stood in front of the cake, swearing.

I rushed over. "What's wrong?" We didn't supply the cake, but maybe one of my guys had bumped it?

She pointed to the elegant script along the base of the cake, Congratulations Courtney and Pete.

"Fuck, fuck, fuck, fuck. It's fucking Brian, not Pete." All the blood seemed to have drained from her face.

I grabbed her arm, afraid she might faint. "So call the bakery. We can wheel it out of here and bring it back after dinner. That will give them two hours to fix it."

She shook her head. "Courtney had me import this from her favorite bakery in San Francisco." Libby pressed a hand to her forehead. "I'm sure I called them about the name change…"

I waved over one of the busboys who were hauling out tables and arranging chairs around them. "Take this cake back to the prep room. And send Kenny over if you see him." I smiled at Libby. "It's going to be okay. I had a pastry class in school. I'm not world-class, but I can fix this."

Kenny appeared at my elbow. He had a beautiful smile. "What's up?"

"Where's the nearest grocery store?"

He thought for a minute. "Mini-mart or big-box?"

"I need cake frosting in a can. Don't care where you get it, but we need it now." I handed him the van keys.

He nodded. "Any particular flavor?"

The cake was decorated in black and white with pink accents and lettering. "Better get me two cans of white frosting and some red food coloring."

Kenny nodded and sprinted off.

Libby shook her head. "Some joker's going to take a photo of the fucking cake and post it online. Shit."

"Stop worrying and give us a hand with the linens. With Kenny gone we're going to be pushed to get the space flipped before people start wandering in."

We set the last napkin in place maybe five minutes before the hordes arrived. Kenny appeared and thrust a plastic grocery bag into my hand. I put Cheryl in charge of getting the food into the waiters' hands and focused on the cake. I didn't have any of the proper tools and felt like MacGyver as I used a salad fork to mix frosting and food coloring in a drinking glass. It took three tries to match the exact shade of Pepto-Bismol pink. With a butter knife I peeled Pete off the cake. The operation left a bumpy impression underneath that I smoothed away with the wetted side of my palm. I fashioned a crude pastry bag out of the plastic bag and practiced a few letters on the counter.

Libby appeared at my elbow and whispered, "It's almost time. Hurry."

I frowned at her. "That's not exactly helpful."

"Right." She disappeared.

I took a deep breath, steadied my hand, and squeezed out the letters one by one. I stepped back to look at it and ran into a warm body. It didn't budge. I turned to see Kenny looking over my shoulder at the cake.

"That's not bad." His chest pressed into my back. My pulse picked up. I didn't want to move away.

Evidently neither did he. We stood looking at the cake for a good thirty seconds. I realized I was holding my breath. I exhaled and shifted forward. "Whether it's okay or not, it will have to do. Libby's going to have a heart attack if I don't get this cake out there soon."

I wheeled the cake out of the staging room. Libby trotted from across the room as I gestured for a busboy to help me lift it onto the table.

A few guests looked up, but most seemed absorbed in their dinner-table conversations. The crease between Libby's eyebrows softened as she took in my work—I'd added a few embellishments to Courtney's name, hoping to hide any calligraphic differences.

She closed her eyes and sighed. When she opened them, she smiled warmly and whispered, "I owe you."

I shrugged. "My pleasure."

Pleasure. That's what I'd felt with Kenny pressed against my back. And fear. I disappeared into the prep area to supervise the changing of the plates.

* * * *

On Tuesday afternoon, after we'd cleaned up from a corporate lunch, Kenny lingered in my doorway.

"Are we still on for tomorrow night?"

I scrunched up my face. "Is this really a good idea? I am your boss."

He cocked his head. "You want me to quit?"

"Would you?"

The creases around his eyes deepened with his smile. "Not on the first date."

"What don't you do on the first date?" Why was it with him I always felt two beats behind?

He grinned. "So this is a date. Good. On the first date I draw the line at quitting my job. At least until after I know if it's worth it."

My mouth went dry, and the rest of me woke up. I held his gaze. "Tomorrow night, then."

He nodded. "Right. The play's at eight, we can eat after, so I'll pick you up at your place at seven thirty?"

It was crazy how my body was responding to him. I pictured us out together at a restaurant after the theater. We'd be giving off that whole first-date vibe—all that sexual energy. I shook my head. That was too public.

Kenny frowned. "I am not going to the theater on the back of your bike. Helmet hair."

"That's not what I meant. Yes, you can pick me up, but let's not go out to dinner."

"Okay." He had an amazing smile. "See you tomorrow."

I was way too messed up for a nice guy like him. I should have warned him, but the big head didn't always win. Ignoring the lingering smell of hay and manure that always accompanied excitement, I glanced at the clock. Twenty-seven hours seemed like a very long time.

* * * *

It took me less than an hour to clean the apartment. That was one of the joys of keeping things sparse. I scrubbed the bathroom, swept the floor, and changed the sheets. I kept telling myself to call him, to cancel the whole thing. I was stepping into a minefield.

But my body had a different idea. It hummed along, fluffing pillows and checking the bureau for supplies. The best I seemed able to do was to vow to be nice to Kenny at work no matter what.

I was sick of French cooking and decided there was something poetic about making a Greek meal on a night I hoped to get laid. There it was, out in the open. My sole goal for my date with Kenny was sex. He was a nice guy with a terrific ass, and I was lonely. A relationship was out of the question, but he might be up for a friends-with-benefits thing. I could handle that. Maybe. As long as it wasn't too public. I suppressed the twinges of guilt I felt over using him by telling myself Kenny was a big boy. He could choose for himself.

I found a nice feta at the neighborhood market, along with frozen phyllo dough and lamb for flaky spinach pie and kebabs. If that didn't impress him, nothing would. I picked up a dark blue tablecloth and matching napkins, a box of candles, some good wine, a Spanish Ribero del Duero, and when I got home I set the table and dug out my grandmother's candleholders. The tiny table on the balcony looked ready to entertain.

I showered, shaved, and stared into the mirror, wishing myself younger and thinner. I had what a one-night stand had called "good bone structure" and all my hair. If there was gray in there, it wasn't yet visible—a benefit of being blond. I'd been with worse. Hopefully so had Kenny.

I rummaged in my closet, looking for clothes I didn't own, clothes that would make me look hip and sexy. I reminded myself that Kenny saw me every day at work. He wasn't expecting Adonis. I put on my blue silk shirt, the one that Anne used to say brought out my eyes, black jeans, and a pair loafers left over from the days when my wardrobe was worth serious cash.

By the time Kenny pulled up to the front door in his battered yellow Bug, I'd almost talked myself down from the ledge of nervousness I'd ramped up to during the day. I waved from the balcony and shouted that I'd be right down.

Kenny cleaned up well. All in black, an open jacket over a T-shirt and jeans, he looked artsy, hip, and hot. Smiling, he gave me a once-over, the type that would have been accompanied by catcalls in my fraternity. Well, if I'd been a woman, that is.

"Hi, handsome. Don't you look spiffy."

I shook my head. "Flatterer."

I slid into the seat, my knees feeling like they hit my chin.

It was seriously weird to be sitting next to Kenny, who I talked with every day but whom I'd been fantasizing about for the past few hours. There we were, and I couldn't think of a thing to say.

He kept his gaze on the road. "I hope you're okay with experimental theater. These guys can get pretty out there."

"Um, sure. It'll be interesting."

Silence.

I finally managed to get out, "Do you see much theater?"

Kenny shrugged. "My writing group has both playwrights and screenwriters. I've even written a few plays myself. We try to see each other's stuff."

"What made you switch to screenwriting? You didn't just write novels. You got awards."

"That's so cool that you looked me up. The awards were great. The money sucked. I know it sounds like total selling out, and everyone in my MFA program agrees that I'm wasting my potential, but literary fiction doesn't pay the bills." He grinned at me. "As much as I like my boss, I'd love to quit waiting tables and write full-time."

His boss. Right.

"Shit." Kenny looked at me. "I shouldn't have said that. About wanting to quit my job."

"Everyone who works there wants to quit."

Kenny snorted. "You're right about that. Did you hear what Stephan made the regular prep cooks do yesterday?"

I breathed a sigh of relief. Shoptalk—such a comfort in stressful moments. We chatted about kitchen politics for the rest of the drive.

"This doesn't look like the theater district," I said as Kenny parallel parked on a residential street.

"Yeah. I forgot to tell you that it's being staged in a garage."

"Say what?"

"I told you it was experimental."

In the driveway of a regular suburban house two young women sat at a card table. Kenny gave his name. While one of the women dug through a small file box, the other watched us from behind big, dark-framed glasses. I shifted uncomfortably. Being out with Kenny felt very public. Of course, I'd been to the theater with other men before. In New York, Anne and I regularly met other couples for dinner and a show. I'd stand in the lobby, chatting with the other guy while our wives did whatever wives do together. Even if I thought the guy was hot, there wasn't anything scary about that. But with Kenny... Well, no one would imagine he had a wife.

The "theater" at the end of the driveway consisted of two rows of bleachers in front of an open, two-car garage. Kenny sat at the far end of the front bleacher. I followed and sat beside him. The inside of the garage was draped in blue fabric. In the middle of the space sat a table, three chairs, and a large plastic snowman. Other than that, the space was bare.

People began filling the benches. I had to scoot closer to Kenny when a couple squeezed in beside us. I felt impossibly conscious of Kenny's thigh against mine. He sat very still, for once not speaking.

I relaxed as a man dressed in a top hat and tails stepped into the center of the garage and admonished us to turn off our cell phones in preparation for the performance. Once the performance started, no one would be watching us.

What followed didn't make a lot of sense. There appeared to be a banker, a child, and a mysterious woman who was either an angel or the janitor. I eventually gave up and drifted in a sleepy haze, enjoying the warm September evening and the press of Kenny's thigh and shoulder against my own.

I blinked back to consciousness with the applause.

Kenny touched my arm. "Is it okay if we stay for a few and socialize? I need to say hi to my friend. It's her script."

I followed Kenny into a backyard festooned with colored lights hanging from the trees. Someone thrust a plastic cup of wine into my hand. I took a sip, a Chablis. Not great, but not bad.

A woman approached us. She looked to be about fifty, an aging hippie in red velvet and purple lace. She threw open her arms. "I saw you from backstage. I'm so glad you came."

Kenny hugged her. "Wouldn't miss it. I brought my boss, George. He's new in town. Thought I'd show him some culture."

I shook her hand, vaguely embarrassed by the relief coursing through me at Kenny's introduction.

After a few more minutes, Kenny nodded toward the driveway. "Ready?"

I followed him to the car.

Once in, he smiled at me. "What did you think?"

I frowned. "I'm afraid I'm not much of a theater critic. I was a banker, remember?"

Kenny laughed. "I didn't understand a word myself. I think it was supposed to be a coming-of-age story, but I'm only guessing at that because of the kid."

"I thought it was a Christmas story. Like Frosty the Snowman on drugs."

He shook his head. "The author's a sweetheart, but I think she left a few too many brain cells on the Orient Express."

* * * *

Kenny looked around at my apartment. "Did you just move in?"

I shrugged. "I'm not a big clutter person."

He laughed. "I can see that. But you should have told me it was BYOC—bring your own chair. Oh, wait. I'll be right back." He flew out of the apartment. I could hear him clattering down the steps. I walked out on the balcony to look down in the street where he'd parked in front of my building.

"What are you doing?"

He leaned into the car and emerged holding a wine bottle triumphantly like a trophy.

I buzzed him back in, and within seconds he was in my living room, panting from his run up the stairs.

He held out the bottle. "I didn't know what you were making, but this looked good. If it doesn't go with this meal, maybe you'll invite me back and cook something that'll go perfectly with this wine."

I examined the label. A Californian pinot that had won a few awards. And it wasn't cheap.

"I thought about a French wine but decided we could use a night off from all things French." Kenny's words came out in a rush.

I smiled. "Thank you. I've been wanting to try this. Make yourself at home. I'll open it."

While I opened the wine, Kenny surveyed the room. He stared at the bed. "Are we eating in bed? I mean, not that I'm refusing or anything, but shouldn't we at least pretend subtlety?"

Laughing, I almost spilled the wineglass I was passing to him. I pointed toward the balcony. "My dining room."

I stepped onto the balcony and bent to light the candles. Kenny stood in the doorway.

"It's very romantic." He stared at me. "Who knew that his hotness himself, Chef All-Business, went in for candlelit suppers in the moonlight?"

"That's not the moon; it's a streetlight." I moved toward the doorway, intending to start plating food.

Kenny stayed where he was. He tapped my chest with his finger. "I knew there was more to you than meets the eye." Laying his hand flat on my chest, he did one of those lascivious body scans of his. "Although, what meets the eye isn't half-bad either."

Before I could catch my breath, he'd melted back into my apartment.

Later, as we sat in the candlelight eating dinner, after he'd moaned and raved and carried on about the food, Kenny cocked his head and asked, "So, gay, bi, or curious?"

I choked on my sip of wine. "Uh, gay."

His eyebrows rose. "Aren't you full of surprises? After that little slip in the kitchen, it was clear you aren't as straight as you've been pretending. But I figured you for a tourist. Or is your ex-wife's real name Henry?"

I shook my head. "No, Anne. Think of me as a late bloomer."

"Huh. Did it come to you one day? 'Hey, you know what?'" He slapped his forehead. "'I'm not straight—I'm gay.'"

I laughed. "Hardly. I fooled around with a few guys in college, but I come from a very conservative background."

"How'd you do it? I mean, I slept with a girl in high school to see what I was missing, but day after day, night after night?" He shook his head.

"It wasn't like I physically couldn't have sex with Anne." He kept looking at me. I could feel myself starting to blush. "Or at least most of the time I could. But neither of us found the experience very satisfying."

"She must have been relieved to find out that particular failure wasn't about her."

"I didn't tell her."

He raised his eyebrows.

I shrugged. "I didn't tell anyone, didn't want to add to the drama. Besides, it would have killed my dad." Or he might have killed me.

Kenny rested his elbows on the table and folded his hands beneath his chin. "Parents are usually more resilient than we think they are. How'd your father react when you finally came out?"

"He died later that year, so the issue never came up." I looked down at the street and concentrated on my breathing.

Kenny's voice was soft. "And your mom?"

"She doesn't know." I stood. "Are you done with your plate?"

Kenny held his hands up in a gesture of surrender. "Whoa, sorry. Didn't mean to step over any lines."

"Don't worry about it." I walked the plates into the kitchen. This whole date thing was a very bad idea.

I didn't hear him come in. Two arms wrapped around my waist, and a warm chest pressed against my back.

Kenny whispered, "I've been wanting to touch you from the first day I saw you." He kissed my neck, and my whole body jolted awake. I leaned into him, tilting my head to expose as much of my neck as possible. Kenny emitted a little sigh and ran his tongue in a long, smooth line from my collarbone to my ear. I could feel him hardening against the flesh of my upper thigh.

He slid one hand into my waistband. His finger flicked the tip of my cock, and I twisted in his arms. He grabbed my face with both hands and pulled me into a kiss. I opened to his tongue. I could taste the tang of good wine and feta, and under that his hunger and my own.

Kenny slid his thigh between my legs and backed me up against the counter and he was leaning into me, squeezing my ass cheeks. Zero to ninety in seconds. I thrust against him, my cock aching in my jeans. Kenny's hands were everywhere, and he was moaning into my mouth like a constant conversation.

I pulled away and looked into his eyes, seeing hunger and passion and kindness. The latter almost undid me.

"We should talk about this." I pulled away.

Kenny ran his finger down the same path along my throat that he'd traced with his tongue. "I'm clean. Got tested today. The paper's in my back pocket if you want to check."

I groaned at the sudden image of completely naked sex, something I'd never had. "Last time I got tested was before I left New York."

Kenny began unbuttoning my shirt. The silk moving against my skin lit fires in my nerve endings.

"I don't mean to be disrespectful." Kenny twisted my nipple, which sent a shock of energy straight to my balls. "But maybe you could freshen that up before we do anything drastic."

Freshen up what? The test? Oh. Getting tested, bringing wine for another meal—Kenny was treating this like a new relationship. We needed to have the friends-with-benefits talk. I opened my mouth to speak, and all that came out was a groan as Kenny slid his hand down my pants and grasped my cock.

"Until then, we can improvise."

Fuck it. We could talk later. I shrugged out of my shirt and started unbuttoning my pants.

Kenny strolled to the bed. He tossed aside his jacket, pulled his T-shirt over his head, and was out of his clothing before I could untangle my feet from my shoes, which were stuck in the twist of material around my ankles.

Kenny stood naked and beautiful by my bed.

I let my gaze slide down from his dark chest hair and treasure trail to his thick mat of almost black pubic hair. "You're not a blond."

He laughed and ruffled the spikes on his head. "You didn't seriously think this was real, did you?"

I was staring at his cock, which was long, thick, and curved slightly to the right.

Kenny's voice was lower as he said, "Come here."

I crossed the room in a few strides.

Kenny pushed his hands into my hair. "I like blonds. Why else do you think I'd want to be one?"

I kissed him again. This time I let my hands explore the sleek skin of his back. His muscles felt taut beneath my fingers. He radiated heat, and even though the night was warm, I pressed closer, feeling like I wanted to climb inside him. He moved, and his hard cock slid against mine. As spasms of excitement spiked through me everywhere we touched, I fought down the fear that always came with sex.

Kenny's grip tightened on my hair. He pulled me back a little so he could look into my eyes. "I've been fantasizing about what you said in the kitchen," he whispered. "Maybe I got it wrong, but I think I heard you say"—he leaned close, watching my lips—"that you like having your face fucked."

My mouth dropped open. I closed it. My knees weakened with my relief. We weren't going to have to talk about my sexual neuroses. Not yet. I sank to my knees, peppering his belly with big, openmouthed kisses. His skin smelled spicy, and I relished the way it felt beneath my tongue. He let his hands rest lightly in my hair, constantly talking to me with sighs and moans and movements.

His cock thumped against my chin as my knees hit the floor. He was circumcised, and the head of his penis was a deep, inviting purple. I licked the tip, savoring the sweet-salt taste of him. Then I opened my mouth and let him slowly push in. And in. And in. I opened my throat, trying not to gag.

Kenny pulled out and pushed back in. "Do you really want me to hold your head?"

I nodded, or tried to. With one hand I used his knee to brace myself. Kenny brushed his fingers through my hair a few times and caressed my jaw. I opened wider. He felt incredible. Inhaling the smell of cock, I looked up at him. Our eyes met, and he let out a groan. He stopped caressing the back of my head and held it as he thrust in and out, first slowly, then faster.

My hand went to my own cock. I closed my eyes and concentrated on the feeling of him slamming into my mouth, the moment of fear when he was deep in me, the release when I could breathe again, the abdication of responsibility as he held my head and fucked my mouth harder and harder.

I opened my eyes again when I started to taste him. He was looking down at me, openmouthed, his eyes glazing over. When our eyes met, he started babbling about how gorgeous I was, and oh, baby, take it, and yes, yes, that's it, come for me, baby, come with my cock in your mouth, and oh, I'm gonna come. He pulled back, but I followed, not wanting to let him go, and he spilled into my mouth in long, salty bursts, better than the best red wine. With his cock pulsing in my mouth I stroked myself one more time, and the wave that had been building all day, all month, for most of my life, crashed over me, and I was emptying everything I was onto the hardwood floor between Kenny's feet.

Kenny dropped to his knees and pulled me into a sloppy, cum-sharing kiss.

"There's dessert," I said when I could speak again.

Kenny laughed. "That's what I thought I just had."

We sat cross-legged on the bed with bowls of fresh yogurt drenched in honey. Kenny's naked body was a wonder. There were the colors—dark body hair in stark contrast to his bleached-blond head, his brown eyes, the bruised red of his lips, and his complexion, an intriguing blend of pink and gold. I liked the way his muscles lay beneath his skin, like a waiting lion. I hadn't expected that.

The amazing thing was that he didn't seem to be put off by my body—almost forty, pale, and a little flabby.

Kenny licked honey from the handle of his spoon. I stared at his tongue. He saw me watching. With a smile he ran his tongue along the handle and curled the spoon into his mouth in a move so sensual that my breath caught.

Kenny waved the empty spoon at me. "I can't believe we're here. I've had a crush on you for a long time."

"Me? What about that straight guy you were talking with Cheryl about?"

Kenny blinked at me. "That was you, silly. I thought you were straight. We all did." He rolled his eyes. "I don't know what made us think that. Oh, yeah, maybe the fact you were pretending to be."

I grimaced. "I don't like having my private life talked about in the kitchen. It's no one's business."

Kenny's gaze softened. Shit, I needed to talk to him, tell him I couldn't do a relationship, wouldn't ever move past the quick fuck. I was still trying to figure out a way to say it without hurting him when he put his bowl down and leaned in to kiss me.

His lips brushed mine. Even that light touch felt electric. I pressed forward, wanting more. His mouth opened to my tongue with a sigh. I let my fingers trail across the line of muscle along his upper arm, the one I'd been staring at since we started dessert. Soft skin and hard muscle beneath, like the rest of Kenny it was a study in contrasts. He knee-walked forward, plowing me down to the mattress with the weight of his body. I surrendered myself to his kiss, the way his tongue filled my mouth. He smelled of shampoo and spice and tasted like honey.

He straddled me, his thighs tight against the sides of my hips and our cocks stiffening side by side. Kenny propped himself up on his arms and looked down at me.

"I liked it, what we did earlier. But I'm not really a tough guy in bed. I mean, I'm open and I like to please but—"

I could feel myself blushing as I said, "It's not… I'm not… I don't like to be in control."

His gaze circled my face like a caress, and his voice was gentle. "So you're a bottom?"

"Not exactly. It's hard to explain." Impossible without revealing all my ghosts, which wasn't something I was ready to do. No wonder I never fucked the same man twice.

He whispered, "Try."

I closed my eyes, and I was back in the barn with my father. I whipped them open and focused on Kenny. I moved to get out from under him. "Forget it."

"Wait." He held me where I was, but his voice was soft. "It's okay. Just tell me what you need."

I stared at the clean white line where the wall met the ceiling, shame washing over me in waves. I hated this. The moment when I had to admit that I was a waste of a man. Why had I thought I could finesse it with Kenny? I'd wanted a friend, which made me even more pathetic. I took a deep breath and whispered, "I can't do it unless I'm forced."

"Do I need to hurt you?" His thumbs drew circles on my bicep.

I shook my head.

"Let's give it a try." He leaned down and kissed me, gently at first, then deepening. His hips began to move. I shifted so that his penis stroked mine with every thrust.

"Yeah," he whispered as I squeezed his ass cheeks. Holding himself up with one hand, he ran his other along the length of my side, from my hip to my nipple in a firm sweep that had me bucking into him. His fingers fluttered across my nipple. At the soft tease of his touch I moaned, and he kept doing it. His cock rubbed mine in a way that made me crazy. Kenny's hand left my nipple and crept up to cradle my face, holding me as he pushed his tongue deeper into my mouth. I ran my hands along the smooth flesh of his back, feeling his muscles ripple. I closed my eyes and listened to the slap of our skin and the rustle of sheets, inhaling the spicy smell of him and feeling the slow build of my excitement. Kenny grabbed my hand. He broke our kiss. I watched him lick my palm, his tongue wide and wet. And then his mouth was again on mine, and he pushed my hand between us. I could barely get my hand around our cocks together. Kenny held my wrist as I held our cocks, and we thrust together. I gasped and writhed beneath him, held by his weight, his hand, and his mouth. I could feel his cock stiffen as it wrestled with mine. His breath came in puffs, like he was talking into my mouth, and I felt the slippery wet of his cum on my hand, and it sent me over into a shivering ecstasy that rocked me to my bones.

When I stopped shaking, Kenny rolled to one side. He propped himself on his elbow and looked at me. "Think how much fun we'll have once you get tested."

Sleep pulled at me. I felt vulnerable and worn-out and too tired. We'd need to have the I-don't-do-relationships conversation in the morning. I pulled up the covers, and Kenny crawled beneath, nestling his head on my shoulder as I drifted off to sleep.

* * * *

Sunlight streamed across the floorboards as my eyes flew open. I found myself cuddled against Kenny's back. The clock said six. We had to be at work in two hours. Work. Shit.

I slid out of bed and tiptoed to the kitchen to make coffee, all the while trying to figure out how I was going to get out of the mess I'd made. What had I been thinking?

When I looked back, Kenny was watching me. He nodded toward my doughnut fryer. "Is that a second stove?"

I followed his gaze, acknowledging that the two-foot-square stainless steel box, which with the backing stood over five feet tall, did look like a second stove. "It's a commercial doughnut fryer."

"A side business? What would Stephan say?"

"Nothing like that." I paused, realizing how strange it might sound. But he kept looking at me expectantly, so

I continued, "On my days off I make doughnuts for the neighborhood homeless."

He looked puzzled. "I would have thought you got enough of cooking at work."

I shrugged. It was impossible to explain how good it made me feel to give hurt kids a treat.

Kenny stared at the fryer. "Commercial-grade cooking equipment isn't cheap. That had to cost a couple grand."

"The doughnuts seem to make them happy. And I got it used." For three thousand, but he didn't need to know that. I looked crazy enough as it was.

"Curiouser and curiouser." He was fucking grinning. That was not a good sign. I needed to push him away fast. I tossed coffee beans in the grinder and slammed down the lid. The subsequent whirring saved me from having to speak until I could get my fear under control.

Except it also masked the sound of Kenny coming up behind me.

I jumped when I felt his arms circle my waist. He must have sensed my discomfort, because he stepped back, and when I faced him again, he had a wary look.

He was gorgeous standing naked in the kitchen. I fought an impulse to wrap my arms around him and kiss that look away. Mixed messages, anyone?

"Bagels and coffee okay for breakfast?" I asked, focusing on a spot over his left ear so I wouldn't have to see his expression.

"Sure, whatever." He walked back toward his clothes. As he pulled on his pants and started buttoning his shirt, it felt like I'd lost something. Kenny scooped up one of his shoes from beneath the bed. "I should be getting home anyway."

"Wait." I held out a coffee cup. "Have some breakfast."

He took the cup from me, his eyes narrowed. "Okay."

I concentrated on what I was doing, as if slicing bagels and putting them in the toaster were feats of culinary prowess. "Look, Kenny, last night was great."

He made a sound like he'd been kicked in the stomach.

He squinted at me. "But…"

I fiddled with the toaster. "It's not really a but, more a clarification. I was, um… I hoped, well… What do you think of our being friends with benefits?"

"Friends with benefits. Huh." He blew on his coffee before taking a big sip. "You mean as opposed to boyfriends or instead of a one-night stand." He paused. "I'm just scoping out the terrain."

I buttered a bagel rather than look at him. "I guess instead of either."

"I'm a flirt, but I don't actually sleep around."

"What has that got to do with it?"

He shrugged. "I don't know. Sure, friends with benefits it is."

I handed him the bagel, smiling with relief.

Kenny set his half-finished cup on the counter. Saluting me with the bagel, he strode toward the door. "See you at work. Buddy."

The apartment filled with the echo of his footsteps down the stairs. I went to the balcony to watch him.

As Kenny opened his car door, he looked up. I waved. He gave a curt nod, and he was gone.

* * * *

We had a small catering event scheduled for Friday night—dinner for thirty at a sprawling mansion in the valley. I met Cheryl and the kitchen crew at eight in the morning so we could get the entrées prepped before early afternoon when the restaurant crew was scheduled to arrive.

Cheryl looked like crap. Her eyes were puffy and her face blotched. She'd wrapped a scarf around her head, but errant curls stuck out at odd angles. "It's my daughter. She's in the hospital."

We gathered around her, a tight circle in the staff room. "What happened?" I asked, resting my hand on her arm.

"It's that bastard she's been seeing, the married podiatrist. He dumped her, and she…" Cheryl took a shuddering breath. "She's in the hospital. On suicide watch.

Thank God I found her in time. They stitched up her wrists and…" She squeezed her eyes shut. "Shit. I don't want to cry anymore."

The kitchen erupted with consolations.

"Oh my God, how awful for you."

"Whoa, man, that sucks."

I rubbed my palm in a circle along the tight muscles between her shoulders. "You don't have to be here. We'll be okay. Do you want to go home?"

She shook her head violently. "I want to get out of my head. Besides, I need the money. When she gets out of the hospital, I'll have an uninsured, unmarried, pregnant daughter on my hands."

"Shit," someone whispered.

Cheryl snorted. "Shit is right. I'm gonna be a grandma. How's that for a piece of work?"

The thing I'd learned about hard times was that they came on suddenly, like the earth shifting beneath one's feet. It was like that when my dad died. I was in cooking school at the time. Mom called to tell me he'd had a massive heart attack. One minute I was obsessed with the roux I was stirring, and the next my world changed absolutely. Growing up, I spent plenty of nights lying in bed wishing he'd die. As an adult, my relationship with him was a struggle. And I still wrestled with his ghost. But on that morning and all through my flight to Des Moines, the funeral, and for days afterward, all I could feel was shock.

I gave Cheryl a task chopping and sautéing onions, figuring she could cry all she wanted and no one would think anything of it. Not that any of us would have begrudged her the tears.

As I watched her out of the corner of my eye, I thought about mortality. We were all the blink of an eye away from death or tragedy. I thought about Kenny, of the way his skin smelled like cinnamon, the dark contrast of his eyes, his unexpected muscularity. And his smile. Life was too short to deny oneself pleasure. I made a mental note to find a clinic where I could get tested nearby.

Cheryl worked slowly, and I wasn't about to push her. But as the clock ticked on I tried to compensate by moving as quickly as I could. Even so, we'd just finished loading the van and started on cleanup when the regular crew began to filter in.

With the exception of a couple of prep cooks who floated between crews, I didn't have much contact with the general kitchen staff. But Cheryl had been a line chef for the restaurant crew before the catering venture began. There were whispered conversations that I didn't bother tracking as the restaurant crew pitched in to help us get the kitchen ready for their shift. A few of them kept glancing at Cheryl. It didn't matter that she'd done nothing to elicit their interest and her daughter's problems were nobody's business—in a kitchen gossip is king. Yet another reason why I kept myself to myself. Or I had until the other night.

The bad news was we weren't finished when Stephan strode in, his chest puffed out like a bulldog. He glared at me. "What are you still doing here?"

I squeezed the cloth I was holding so hard it dripped water onto my toe. I hated kowtowing to petty tyrants. Swallowing my first two comebacks, I mumbled, "We'll be out of here in a few minutes."

"Not good enough." He glared at Cheryl. "What do you have to say? You've been here long enough to know how this works. How am I supposed to work with all these people cluttering up my kitchen?"

I moved to block Stephan's view of Cheryl. "Don't blame her. If you need to yell at someone, yell at me. I'm responsible for the catering crew."

His eyes narrowed, and his nostrils flared. "I'll remember that. In the meantime, get this place cleaned up and your people out of here." He turned and stomped back to his office.

I nodded to two prep cooks who stood gawking at me. "You heard him. Let's get this place cleaned up."

They jumped to work. I turned toward Cheryl. "You okay?"

She scowled. "I'm so sorry. That was my fault."

"That Stephan was a dick? Hardly." I wrapped an arm around her shoulders. "Do you want to work the event tonight, or would you rather go home?"

She leaned into me. "She's in the psych ward on lockdown. If it's all right with you, I'd rather work."

Patting her arm, I walked Cheryl toward the van.

* * * *

Cheryl barely spoke during the forty-five-minute drive into the hills. I kept stealing peeks at her. I didn't have children, but I adored my brother's daughter, Jessica. Mind you, I hadn't seen her in years. Keeping my sexuality secret from my family meant I'd cut down on visits. I couldn't imagine what it must be like in Cheryl's head right then.

Kenny, a dishwasher, and another waiter met us at the venue. It was the first time I'd seen him since the morning after our night together. Our eyes locked. I felt the blood surging to my cheeks as my spirits lifted. He looked like sunshine to me.

I checked to see if Cheryl noticed the difference in the way the air vibrated between us, but she was staring straight ahead, lost in thought.

Kenny stepped close to her and touched her elbow. "Are you okay?"

Her eyes filled with tears.

I rested my hand on Kenny's shoulder and whispered, "Why don't you two take a walk. The three of us can get set up. Be back in an hour to help serve."

Kenny held my gaze. I made a little face, hoping to convey that it was bad, really bad, and she needed a shoulder.

He seemed to get it, nodded, and with an arm around Cheryl, led her down the lane, away from the house.

"Okay." I clapped my hands to get the attention of my remaining crew. "Let's move."

Short two pairs of very capable hands, we had to hustle to get dinner set up, but by the time Kenny and Cheryl returned, we were well on our way.

Cheryl's eyes and nose were red, but she held her shoulders back, and she looked stronger, more resolute than she had before they left.

It turned out I really did need her, because the host threw in a last-minute request for L'Ouest puff pastry desserts. There were plenty back in the freezer at the restaurant. I left Cheryl in charge of the kitchen and drove the van at illegal speeds in an hour-long round-trip dash to retrieve them. When I got back, the dinner service was halfway through, and Cheryl had the oven ready to warm up the desserts. As we plated them together, it felt like the finish line of a marathon. Except it was just dinner at some rich guy's house. More fulfilling than selling stocks, but pretty trivial in the grand scheme of things.

It was after ten before we had the kitchen cleaned and our equipment and the garbage loaded back into the van. Catering in private homes was like committing the perfect crime—we erased all evidence that we'd been there.

Cheryl was already in the van when I stopped Kenny outside his little yellow car. "Thanks for taking care of her. I think you made a real difference."

He shook his head. "Poor thing."

I shrugged. "I'm no good at that sort of thing. Don't know what to say."

"You don't need to say anything. Mostly you need to listen." He leaned back against his car, his gaze soft on my face.

I shuffled my feet in the gravel that lay scattered on the pavement. "There's nothing on for work on Sunday. Do you want to come over?"

He tilted his head. In the streetlight his hair looked almost white, like a halo. "Is this a friend thing, a couple of guys watching football? Or are you more interested in the benefits?"

Why was he being so touchy? "I don't know. Can't we get together and see how it goes?"

He shrugged. "Okay. But I don't like football."

"Neither do I."

He smiled. "Guess we'll have to figure out something else to do. Buddy. Maybe I'll bring a deck of cards."

And with that he climbed into his car. As I walked back to the van, I listened to him drive away.

* * * *

This time Kenny arrived holding a pastry box. He was dressed in a worn pair of jeans and a gay-pride T-shirt, and looked scrubbed clean and cheerful. I'd spent the morning obsessing about how to greet him—a handshake, a hug, a kiss?

When the moment came, he sidestepped the issue by thrusting the bakery box toward me. "Here you go, Mr. Doughnut Man. From the new cupcake place on Sunset. I thought you'd want to give them a try."

I opened the door, and Kenny strolled in. He looked around the apartment. "Man, you are going to have to get a couch. The way you've got this place set up, it's all or nothing. No opportunity for nuance."

"We could meet at your place."

He laughed. "Hardly. I have three roommates. Nuance is all that happens there."

"Doesn't writing take privacy? How do you do that with three roommates?"

He shrugged. "Lockable doors."

I opened the box and found a dozen gorgeously decorated cupcakes. "I made coffee. We can sit on the balcony."

"If you like."

The room seemed to crackle with sexual energy. I was half-hard from a morning thinking about Kenny. I looked at his crotch. Those pants weren't lying flat, and as I watched, the bulge seemed to grow. I looked up to see Kenny watching me.

My test results. I set the box on the kitchen counter, dug a slip out of my back pocket, and thrust it at him.

Kenny held the paper with two hands and read. He looked up. "Maybe you should pour that coffee, George. We should talk."

"About what?"

Kenny passed so close beside me that I could feel his heat. He picked up the pastry box and leaned in so his face was inches from mine. I thought he might kiss me. Instead, he whispered, "You bring the coffee. I've got these."

I watched him stroll through my balcony door. The way his ass moved when he walked had me fantasizing about his naked skin. I picked up two cups, poured coffee—black for myself, cream with two sugars for Kenny—followed him out to the patio, and sat down in the seat he'd left for me.

Kenny propped his feet on the railing and leaned back in his chair. "It's nice out here."

"It was god-awful hot last month, but today isn't bad." I sipped my coffee and waited for Kenny to start talking about whatever it was he wanted to talk about. Me, I was ready to go back inside and get naked.

Kenny blew on his coffee and took a sip. He looked at me over the rim of his cup. "You're a confusing guy, George Zajac, do you know that?"

No shit, Sherlock. You should try it from the inside. I shrugged.

He opened the box, picked up one of the cupcakes, ripped it in two, and handed me the slightly larger piece. "I can live with ambiguity. Keeps me on my toes. The thing is, I think we need to establish a few ground rules for this friends-with-benefits thing."

I licked the frosting. They'd used real butter in the buttercream. Kenny was watching, his eyes riveted by my tongue. I took another long lick. He swallowed. I smiled and nodded for him to go on.

He held up the paper I'd handed to him. "First, are you planning on sleeping with anyone else? Because if you are, this paper doesn't mean anything after today."

I wrinkled my brow. It was exciting to imagine having sex with the same person on a regular basis and not having to explain myself over and over. The idea of breaking in someone new sounded exhausting. On the other hand, I didn't want Kenny to the get wrong idea and think we were getting into a real relationship. I cleared my throat. "There's no one else at the moment."

Kenny nodded. "But we're not exclusive, right?"

The image of Kenny with someone else made me very uncomfortable. "Right."

"So, rule number one is that we tell the other if we're going to have sex, or have had sex, with anyone else."

"Fair enough." I popped the rest of the cupcake in my mouth, savoring the rich chocolate of the cake itself. I'd need to contact the bakery and see if they did wedding cakes.

"Rule number two." Kenny held up two fingers. "By definition, friends with benefits means either one of us can decide we're not having sex anymore and the other can't get pissed off. Because we're friends, right?"

"Right." Except if Kenny said he didn't want to have sex this afternoon, I'd be fucking pissed.

He held up three fingers. "No jealousy, possessiveness, or behavior unbefitting of a friend, right?"

"Okay." All these rules. But he was probably right.

Kenny smiled and crammed his half of the cupcake into his mouth. Around a mouthful of cupcake, he said, "Good. Hmm? They make wedding cakes too."

In one swift movement, Kenny scooped up another cupcake and twirled from his chair to straddle my lap. He pulled off a bite of cake and pushed it into my mouth.

I looked down at the road—it was relatively empty for a Sunday afternoon.

Still. "Let's go inside."

He leaped off and stood, eating the rest of the cupcake. He watched me get up, straighten my chair, and pick up the coffee cups.

"This is Los Angeles." Carrying the cupcakes, he followed me in. "Nobody cares, George."

I put the coffee cups on the kitchen counter. "I don't like everyone knowing my business."

"What business is that, George? Your catering business?"

I folded my arms and glared at him. "I'm not the type to flaunt it."

Kenny frowned. "Flaunt it? Interesting word choice. Been watching televangelists, have you?"

Christ. That hit too close to home. I deliberately uncrossed my arms. "Look, Kenny. It's complicated. I'm a Midwesterner from a religious background. We don't do public displays of affection." Especially with very gay members of the same sex.

Kenny blew out a puff of air. "Sorry, I guess I'm sort of sensitive. I got a lot of shit for being gay in high school. You know how crappy kids can be."

I nodded.

"My best friend Nathan and I used to practice swaggering—you know, that whole stiff-legged straight-guy walk. He sort of got it, or at least as much as a science nerd needed to. I never could."

I stepped closer, meaning to pat his arm or back or make some sort of sympathetic gesture.

Kenny whirled away. He held the cupcake box high and sashayed toward the bed. "But you know what they say. Living well is the best revenge. And now they're all stuck back in windy Chicago, while I live in Los Angeles where there are plenty of good cupcakes and hot men." He kicked off his sandals and settled onto my bed.

He was right. We weren't in the Midwest anymore. And as for hot men, Kenny looked incredibly sexy lying on my bed, watching me from under long dark lashes. He held up a cupcake. "Want more? Now that we have the rules down for this friendship, maybe we can explore some of those benefits."

He didn't have to ask me twice.

We only ate one cupcake in bed. Kenny peeled off the skirting and held it between us so we could eat our way toward each other. When our lips met, he tasted of chocolate and buttercream. Without breaking the kiss, he shoved the cupcake box out of the way. Crumbs fell between us, but I didn't care. With any luck I'd need to change the sheets soon anyway.

Even through his T-shirt I could feel the heat from Kenny's skin. His scapulas felt like wings. Kenny held my face in his hands and kissed me deeply. I slid my hands down his back to cup his ass. I pulled him against me. The bulk of his cock pressed against my thigh. I rubbed mine against his belly, both of us hard and ready.

Kenny pulled away, but he didn't let go of my face. He smiled, his eyes warm on my own. "I know you don't like to be in charge, Mr. Always Really in Charge. But your little paper says we can do anything we like—alfresco, as it were. I'd like to know what you like."

I pictured the round globes of Kenny's ass beneath his jeans. "I, um, I want to pitch."

Kenny's eyebrows rose. "That wasn't what I expected. I mean, given everything else. But it works for me." He pulled off his T-shirt. "You're a complicated guy."

I started yanking on my own clothes, trying to get them off as quickly as possible. "What? Just cause I'm not a control freak, you think I can't—"

Kenny laughed. "Whoa, boy. Careful. I'm not saying anything except that you're complicated." He wrapped his naked self around my back as I bent to pull my pants off. "I never said I liked simple."

Kenny's lips were warm on the base of my neck. The blood was rushing out of my brain and into my cock. I couldn't think of anything witty or interesting to say and leaned back into him. He tugged me down, still pressed against my back, his tongue running the length of my neck and up beneath the back of my ear. His cock slid between my legs and rubbed against my balls. I had to talk to him. I was glad I couldn't see his face.

"Look…" I paused, too embarrassed to keep going.

"Tell me," he whispered into my neck.

I took a deep breath. "I-I need you to force me to fuck you."

Kenny pulled away. He rolled me onto my back and looked into my face. "Seriously?"

I nodded. This was it—the moment he'd either walk away or turn into a total dick. The kindness of his gaze was hard to take. Mortified, I looked away.

He kissed me. "Where's the lube?"

I nodded toward the bedside table. Kenny broke away long enough to pull open the drawer and find it, and then he was back, kissing me. He dropped the lube on the pillow beside my head and ran his hands down my arms to where I was gripping his thighs. Kenny grabbed both my wrists and brought my hands above my head, holding me down as he kissed me deeper. I thrust against him, my cock pushing against his. I was so hard I could feel myself leaking across his belly. Or maybe that was him.

Kenny held my hands with one of his and reached for the lube. He flipped the top open and thrust the bottle into my hands. "Hold that. Now squeeze it."

I squeezed until he told me to stop. I could feel my hands shaking as I clutched the bottle above my head.

Kenny sat on my thighs and lubed my cock. He made me squeeze the bottle again and reached around to finger his ass. By the time he got to his knees and positioned himself over me, I was drenched in sweat.

He touched my arm. "Let go of the bottle. I want your hands on my ass."

I dropped the lube and clasped his ass cheeks. Kenny winced as he pushed himself onto me. He felt hot and tight. I could barely breathe. He stayed there, with only the tip of my cock buried in his ass, until I felt his muscles relax.

With a moan he slid down me, and I was engulfed in that tight heat. I ground my fingers into the flesh of his ass as he road up and down on my cock. His thigh muscles flexed. Sweat trickled down his chest, and his face twisted until he looked like a tortured angel. My breath came in ragged huffs in time with the slap of his ass against my balls.

"I'm close," I gasped.

His hand flew to his cock. With each breath, each thrust, my world shrank to the feel of Kenny's ass around me, engulfing me, keeping me safe. Blood pounded in my ears. I was scrambling at the covers with my legs, trying to bury myself deeper into him, to climb inside him. Kenny cried out. The sight of his cock spurting in a giant arch onto my chest sent me panting, clawing, and groaning, spilling myself into him like secrets.

Kenny leaned forward, coming off me with a pop. He propped himself over me with a hand on either side of my head. "That was… I don't even know how to describe it. You're twisted, but you're fucking hot."

I grimaced. "I know. I'm fucked up."

His gaze was soft. "You're okay." He rolled onto his back. "Gotta tell you, I like the friendship, but the benefits are amazing."

2005: A December Wedding

This one was to be massive, a three-course meal for five hundred. It would take us at least a day ahead of the wedding to set up the banquet hall. Even though the wedding was more than a week away, Cheryl and the kitchen crew were already working full-time on the one event, which the tabloids were calling the wedding of the year.

"There will be photographers all around," Stephan announced, his chest puffed out like a pastry. "If there is press, I will talk to them."

"You'll be there?" That would be a first. Not that I expected him to help. He'd only show up to hoard the media attention.

"Of course. I cannot leave the restaurant until a few minutes before the event, but I will be there to supervise."

Supervise my crew? I bit my tongue. Stephan had let people go with less provocation than that. Could he be more self-aggrandizing? I wasn't sure how much longer I'd be able to stand it. If it hadn't been for Kenny, I'd have already moved on.

I marched back to the kitchen to give Cheryl the bad news. "His Highness says he intends to grace us with his presence at the wedding."

"Shit." She looked up from the sauce she was stirring. "As if we didn't already have enough stress."

"Are you worried about your daughter? I can shift people around so she doesn't have to work that night."

"Are you kidding? She'd kill me if she didn't get to serve at, and I'm quoting Tattler, 'the most lavish Hollywood wedding since Tori Spelling's.' Not that that's much of an endorsement for the marriage."

"All the more reason for us to do such a stellar job that they both want us for their next weddings." I checked the pan of onions one of the prep cooks was sautéing. "Give that five more minutes before you start the next batch," I told her before turning back to Cheryl. "She seems to be doing well."

"Thanks for talking Chef into giving her a job." Cheryl smiled. "She's got a good counselor. And I think now that she's getting used to the idea, the prospect of the baby actually helps. Or at least she seems excited about it."

Checking the menu again, I asked, "This is mostly our standard fare, but how do you supposed Libby got Stephan to sign off on figgy pudding? It's not exactly French."

Cheryl shrugged. "I think he's a little starstruck by the whole affair." She dipped a spoon into the sauce vierge and held it out to me. I tasted, nodded, and she began pouring it into the waiting containers. We wouldn't be putting together the final dishes until the day before the wedding.

Cheryl didn't look at me as she asked, "I haven't seen Kenny around lately. What's going on with him?"

"He took a few days off. A theater in West Hollywood is reading one of his plays at the end of the month. It's a one-night thing, part of a new playwright series. This is his week to meet with the director and cast. He's pretty excited about it."

"That's great. When's the play? We should all go."

"The twenty-eighth. I'm sure he'd love it if a bunch of people from here went."

Cheryl dropped butter into her pan to start the next batch of sauce. She peered at me. "You seem to have grown close over the past few months."

"He's a great guy." I tried to sound nonchalant, despite the blush I could feel creeping up my face.

"He's a sweetheart. I'd sure like to see him find the right guy." She stared into the pan as she spoke.

I leaned across the counter and lowered my voice. "We're friends, Cheryl. That's all."

Her eyes were sad as they met mine. "Got it. None of my business."

I punched the brioche dough harder than I should have. She was right. It wasn't any of her business what kind of friends Kenny and I were. So what if we spent most nights together? That was what friends did, wasn't it?

Cheryl broke the silence with, "So anyone want to make bets on how long this marriage will last?"

I blinked at her. It took me a minute to realize she wasn't talking about Kenny anymore. One of the prep cooks suggested two years, another three months, and within minutes the betting pool was on. I was an optimist, so I went for the long odds and guessed until death did them part.

* * * *

And then everything went to hell. My brother Al called me at seven thirty Sunday morning, the weekend before the wedding. He was on his way to church. I was making Kenny coffee.

"Hey, bro." One of the reasons he'd done so well as a used car salesman was that voice, all hail-fellow-well-met. His cheerful manner had flagged for a while after his wife had died three years before. Now he was back to sounding like himself, a nice guy who took fantastic care of the women in his life—our mom and my favorite and only niece, Jessica.

"Hi." Kenny tried to pull me back in bed as I handed him his coffee, but I moved away and paced to the kitchen counter. Al rarely called, and I wasn't about to let him know there was a man in my bed. "What's up?"

"We're coming out to sunny California. What do you think of that?"

My stomach tightened. I liked my life to stay compartmentalized, me in LA and them in the cornfields. Otherwise things could get messy. Still, I liked my brother. "Where in California? It's a big state."

He laughed. "Like we'd come out there and not hit Los Angeles. Jess and I are taking Mom to Disneyland to celebrate her seventieth. Give her a head start on her second childhood."

Right. I hadn't even thought about Mom's birthday. I could add bad son to my list of failings. "Wow. When?"

"After Christmas. We can visit you, check out your life and that fancy restaurant where you work, and catch the fireworks at Disneyland on New Year's Eve. Start the new year right."

I was watching Kenny, who was sipping his coffee and watching me. It's not like I could tell my brother, You know, that's a bad week for me because my friend has a show. I said, "That sounds great."

"I'll let you know the details later. Gotta run now. We're pulling up to the church." He paused. "Mom says she's printed out a list of churches for you to try. Mom, he's a grown man. He doesn't need your help in that department. Gotta go, bro. Talk with you again soon."

As I said good-bye, Kenny asked, "Another holiday party?"

I shook my head. "Worse. My family is coming to visit."

"Cool. We'll have to have a party. Everyone will want to know where George came from."

I frowned at him. "No parties. And here's the thing. They're coming during the week of your show."

He beamed. "Great. I'll comp you tickets. The best way to ensure an audience is to bring your own."

"I can't take my mother to see your play." I sat on the bed next to him.

"Why not? It's not obscene or anything. I told you, it's a straight love story."

"It's not that. I can't risk it. She doesn't know. She can't know. Mom's a very religious person." I was sweating, again remembering that damned smell of manure. "The church my family goes to—New Pentecostal, the one I grew up in—Anne used to say it was an inch from snake handling, and she was right."

"I promise there's nothing in there that will offend her. What are you worried about?" He watched me not answer for a few moments as I thought about my mother meeting Kenny, the look of horror on her face when she realized he was gay, and the sinking feeling in my stomach her disgust would produce. Kenny continued, "We're friends, right? That's what you keep insisting. So why can't you take your mother to your friend's new play?"

He could be so infuriatingly logical. "Because she'll know you're gay."

He shrugged. "Maybe. But she won't know you are. I'm not going to kiss you in front of your mother." He stood and started getting dressed. "I know your rules, George, and I've gotten good at playing them, if I do say so myself."

I put an arm out to stop him. "Don't get mad. I didn't mean—"

"I know what you mean, probably better than you do yourself. I gotta go. I promised the director I'd take a look at his suggested revisions today."

"Kenny, you're being unreasonable." I stood and followed him to the door.

"I don't think so." He stopped, his hand on the doorknob. "It's up to you. I'd love to have you at the show, but if you're too afraid of what your mother might think about your gay 'friend,' then that's the way it is."

Shit. I'd hurt his feelings again. I wished he wouldn't be so damned sensitive. "Are you coming back tonight?"

Kenny sighed. "Yeah. Maybe. I'll call you later."

After he left, I stood in the empty apartment staring at the door. Fuck him for getting in a snit about it. I closed my eyes and was back in the barn with my father. My heart pounded. No matter what, they could never know.

* * * *

"It's so weird to me to see Christmas decorations and people walking around in shirtsleeves," I told Cheryl. We were on our way to the venue to start setting up for the star-studded gala.

"Hey, it's long shirtsleeves, so what do you want?"

I passed a Santa in shorts. "Snow?"

She wrinkled her nose. "Sleigh bells ringing—all that crap?"

"Not a Christmas fan?"

"No. Not a fan at all. When I was a kid, Christmas was a time to fend off drunken uncles. I tried to make it nice for my kids, but it always felt flat for me."

"We had great Christmases in Iowa. My folks went all out with the tree. And my mom baked the best cookies. My mom's birthday is the day before Christmas, and my dad always made a big deal about it. The whole week was kind of special. I have great memories of decorating sugar cookies, drinking hot chocolate, and sledding with Al."

"Sounds like Norman Rockwell come to life."

I shrugged. "One week out of the year."

"So why don't you go back there for Christmas? Why don't I ever hear about your family, for that matter?"

"I left home at eighteen and haven't gone back much. Anne hated my family, and my dad and I didn't get along. He's gone now, but I guess I never developed the habit of going home."

"And here I was picturing you with the perfect white-bread family." She cocked her head and considered me. "This year they'll be out here. What are you going to do?"

I looked out at the un-Christmassy Christmas landscape. "I don't know."

"A bunch of us are going to Kenny's play. Maybe you and your family could join us."

I sighed. "Did he put you up to asking me?"

She shook her head. "No. But he did say he hoped you'd come. You mean a lot to him."

I stared at her. "What did he tell you?"

"Nothing I hadn't already figured out for myself."

"I don't like being gossiped about." I slammed the brakes too hard as I pulled into the parking space. The van jolted to a stop.

"Then quit being an idiot. Come to the damned play." Cheryl leaped out, and the door banged shut.

I climbed down from the seat ready to argue but stopped when I saw the cluster of my employees coming toward the van. The argument would have to wait.

Kenny was already inside arranging chairs. He glanced up at my entrance, nodded curtly, and went back to what he'd been doing.

A couple of bussers jumped as I barked at them to get a move on with the tablecloths. Everyone seemed to be angry with me. Which was just fine. It wasn't like I needed their approval. I went back outside to supervise unloading the van.

* * * *

"More stars than in the heavens," Cheryl murmured as we watched the wedding guests wander into the banquet hall. With a slight incline of her head, she gestured toward a distinguished-looking older man. "Is that who I think it is?"

Beside her Kenny looked sexy in the black pants and scarlet vest the bride had ordered for every waiter. He whispered, "I think so. Didn't he play the groom's father in that sports film last year?"

Cheryl nodded. "I think you're right."

Beside those two I felt like a cultural moron. The only movie I'd seen either of the happy couple in was a made-for-TV special where the bride played a single mom with a fatal disease. After that it was disconcerting seeing her glide into the room in a long white gown that showed off her pale, thin shoulders and exposed each of her vertebrae to the candlelit room. At her side the groom was breathtaking in an old-fashioned dove-gray top hat and tails. I looked over at Kenny to see what he thought of the happy couple, but he was engrossed in whispered conversation with Cheryl about the guests as they drifted around, searching for their seats.

We stood at attention behind the food table, dozens of waiters and a phalanx of chefs waiting for the signal to serve. At the head of our line Stephan preened like a proud parent, despite the fact he'd shown up at the last minute, not having lifted one chair, chopped a vegetable, or contributed to the presentation of a single platter.

On the other side of Kenny stood Cheryl's daughter, still thin and pale with the hint of a baby bump, but much less fragile than she'd been when she started the month before. We all stood tall, and the place felt regal. At a signal from Libby, I whispered, "Go." The crew flew out into the hall, carrying platters of salad plates in a coordinated dance that impressed even me. Cheryl plated the fish, I carved beef, and Stephan looked important.

Halfway through the meal I noticed Libby beaming from across the room. I smiled back. It was times like that, when the whole crew felt in the groove and everything flowed like magic—that's when I loved my job.

During dessert, the bride and groom worked the room, spending a few minutes at each table. It was like watching royalty. As they passed our station, Stephan sputtered on obsequiously. The groom rolled his eyes, and it occurred to me I was witnessing the only glitch in an otherwise perfect evening. I tried not to scowl.

I was married for ten years. For most of that time we were pleasant, if distant. But I'd never looked at Anne like these two looked at each other. They made me believe in true love. Or at least in the illusion of true love—they were actors, after all.

Stephan left soon after his fawning visitation and before the long night of cleanup began. The bussers cleared away the food. Cheryl and I dismantled our stations, the waiters filled their trays with glasses of champagne, and the party moved from sedate to rambunctious.

I sent Cheryl home and ducked into the kitchen to supervise cleanup. I was gesturing toward a washed crate of dishes that needed to be loaded into the van when I felt a touch on my arm. I turned to find the groom at my elbow.

"Can I help you, sir?" I asked, noting how startlingly blue his eyes were.

He gestured for me to follow him into the hallway between the kitchen and the banquet hall, where he leaned against a wall and lit a cigarette. "Don't say it. I know I'm not supposed to smoke in here, but I'm dying."

Far be it from me to tell the client what he could and couldn't do. "Do you want me to get you an ashtray?"

He shook his head and held up his empty champagne glass. "Got it covered. I just wanted to say—"

A busser with a tray full of glasses approached. I stepped out of the way, which took me within inches of the groom. All I could think was that I was closer to a movie star than I'd ever expected to be. That would be a story to tell my mom when she arrived.

"Just wanted to say that the food was fantastic. Thank you."

I nodded. "I'm glad you're pleased."

He dropped his cigarette into the glass. It sputtered out. He reached into his pocket and brought out folded bills, which he pressed into my palm. Holding my hand for the kind of moment that would mean something if I hadn't seen him use the same earnest gesture on dozens of people around the room, he said, "Libby says you're the best. Your boss is a dick. Let me know if you ever venture out on your own."

He handed me the cigarette-filled glass, turned on his heel, and disappeared out the door. He had to pass Kenny on the way out. Kenny was standing a few feet inside the door with a funny look on his face.

I waved him over. "I think I just got a tip."

He shouldered his tray of glasses and stepped closer. "I've got a tip for you. Don't date married men."

"Very funny. Look at this." I opened my hand to show him a wad of cash. I started counting. "There's a couple thousand dollars here. Even with as many of us as there were tonight, we'll all go home with a chunk of change."

He wasn't looking at the money. He was looking at me. "He's gorgeous up close, isn't he?"

"Sure, that's his job." I held Kenny's gaze. "Will you stop being mad at me?"

"I'm not mad. Disappointed, but not mad." He shifted his weight onto the other foot. That tray was probably getting heavy.

I closed my eyes. What the hell. Cheryl was probably right. When I opened them, I said, "Okay, we'll go to the play. As long as you promise not to shock my mother."

His mouth curved into that heartbreakingly eager smile that always got me. "Really? That's great—I promise."

He looked like he might kiss me.

I sidestepped the gesture. There'd be time for that later, when we were really alone.

* * * *

What with company parties and society dos, we were balls to the wall from the second week in December until Christmas Eve. My family was due in town the day after Christmas. It seemed way too boyfriend-y to spend Christmas with Kenny, no matter how much he protested that it was just another day.

He lay in my bed on the morning of Christmas Eve looking tousled and gorgeous. "I'll be catching a movie and eating Chinese, like every other Jew in town. You're welcome to join me."

I declined and sent him home. I'd have liked his company but didn't want to give him the wrong impression. We might spend almost every night together, but holidays, those were for relationships.

On Christmas Eve night, I sat at my balcony table listening to five different kinds of Christmas songs coming from apartments below, above, and across the street. Colored lights hung from palm trees. Lit Christmas trees filled the windows of several apartments I could see from my balcony. The night was cool enough to warrant a sweatshirt.

I thought about Cheryl's daughter and her married man. Loneliness and desperation could make people do crazy things. I wondered if I'd ever have a regular life, one where pretty wrapped packages were exchanged on cold, crisp mornings while snow fell outside and a fire crackled in the hearth. And would there be someone special to share them with, or would the wild craziness of my childhood haunt me forever in wounds that never healed?

I drank too much wine and fell asleep. The next morning I hopped on my bike and rode the deserted, sun-drenched highways of Los Angeles until the empty feeling went away.

* * * *

By happy coincidence, the catering calendar was empty from Christmas until the day before New Year's Eve, which left me free to escort the family around town. I might have enjoyed spending days on end in bed with Kenny, exploring his skin with my tongue, but that wasn't in the cards. In fact, I planned not to see him except for the night of the play. Even though Mom and Al and Jessica would be staying somewhere else, I couldn't risk an overnight with Kenny while they were in town.

Since my place consisted of one room, a king-size bed, and not much else, I made a reservation for the family at a nearby hotel—nothing fancy, the kind of place where they leave the light on. Since I couldn't carry everyone on my bike, I rented a midsize car for the visit. In New York we would have taken public transportation, but this was LA, where the highway was king.

I parked the rental and navigated LAX until I stood outside security for their gate. The day after Christmas, the place bustled with the muffled clamor of thousands of holiday travelers. Families parted and greeted, and lovers of all genders kissed hello and good-bye. I couldn't picture myself hugging a man in an airport, oblivious to what anyone else thought.

Mom appeared looking smaller than I remembered, a short, round woman in a baby-blue tracksuit. I tried to ignore the sense of my father's ghost that tickled my attention when I saw her. Beside her, my older brother looked like an aging football player, with broad shoulders and the hint of a belly drooping over his belt. He saw me and bounded over, engulfing me in a huge hug. We were the same height, same build and coloring. Which was why the scattering of gray by his temples was disconcerting. As I leaned down to hug my mother, I inhaled her familiar scent—talcum powder, vanilla, and inexpensive perfume. When I straightened, I was greeted by a thin blonde woman with my father's coloring and her mother's eyes.

"Jessica, you're all grown up." I realized with a pang that I hadn't seen her, or my brother, since Dad's funeral. Three years is a long time for a kid, although she wasn't a kid anymore. She'd be nineteen. "Hey, how's that fancy college of yours?"

"Did we tell you?" My brother beamed at his daughter. "Jess is the first sophomore to ever be editor of the school newspaper."

"Dad." She smiled up at Al. "Can the bragging wait?"

He put his arm around her and pulled her into a jostled side hug. "Sorry, honey. Can't help it."

My mother patted Jessica's arm. "We're all proud of you, dear. Aren't we, George?"

"Yes, of course." Not that I knew her anymore. But she was the Zajac family's only shot at another generation. I gestured down the terminal. "Luggage?"

* * * *

After I got them settled in their hotel, my mother insisted on seeing where I lived. As we trooped up the stairs, I couldn't help comparing my clean but shoddy building to the high-rise I left behind in New York. The last time my mother visited my apartment, I had a doorman and a view of Central Park. I was also desperately unhappy, but she hadn't known that. So I wondered what she'd think of my new, much-reduced status.

"Whoa, bro." Al whistled as he entered the space. "It looks like you just moved in."

"That's what Kenny said." It came out before I could stop myself.

My mother looked at me sharply. "Who's Kenny?"

I gritted my teeth. Me and my big mouth. "A friend, a guy I work with."

"I like it." Jessica stood in the center of the room and turned around in a slow circle. "It's very Zen."

My mother ran a hand along the kitchen counter. "Not to mention efficient. Cleaning must be a snap." She stared at the bed. "Do you live here alone?"

"Of course." I gestured around me. "Not room for anyone else."

"That's too bad." She stepped into the bathroom. Since she didn't close the door I assumed it was part of the inspection tour. "I hate to think of you lonely out here, so far from home."

I laughed nervously. "I work a lot. I don't have time to be lonely."

She emerged from the bathroom with a smile. "That's nice, dear. How about lunch?"

* * * *

The Magic Kingdom was more crowded than magic, and the Paramount Pictures tour gave me a headache. Still, it was nice to spend time with my family. Mom seemed unchanged. Al was back to his old self—the cheerful guy I'd known before his wife died. Every now and then I'd catch him staring off into space, a haunted look around his eyes, but the majority of the time he was jovial. I found myself really enjoying my niece. Back when I'd seen her more often, she'd been a fun kid, always up for an adventure. That giggly girl still showed up, but mostly she'd been replaced by a mature young woman. She was interested in politics. When I stopped reading the Wall Street Journal, I'd quit following current events. Jessica brought me up to speed. She was much more liberal than her dad. That was interesting too.

* * * *

The night of Kenny's play, we met Cheryl and her daughter before the show. I told myself it might be nice for Jessica to talk with someone her own age, and that since Cheryl was the closest thing to a friend I'd made in Los Angeles—other than Kenny, of course—it was only natural I wanted my family to meet her. That she might provide me some cover was an added bonus.

While the girls talked about music and favorite television shows, my mother pumped Cheryl for recipes, something she hadn't done with me in the entire four years I'd been a professional chef.

Al asked, "So what's this play?"

"It's a staged reading. Evidently there won't be moving around. It's a chance for new writers to get their plays seen."

Al nodded. He took a sip of his scotch on the rocks. "And someone you work with wrote it?"

"Kenny, he's one of the waiters."

Mom broke in. "Yes, you've mentioned him."

Jessica smiled across the table. "More than once."

My heart thudded. Shit. Why couldn't I ever keep my mouth shut?

Cheryl spoke. "The three of us spend a lot of time together at work."

Mom was looking from me to Cheryl, her face intent with concentration. "With your hours it must be very difficult to have a social life outside of work."

Cheryl laughed. "You got that right. I haven't had a date in years."

There went my cover. Fortunately, Jessica changed the subject.

* * * *

I don't think I breathed through the whole first act of Swamp Dancing: A Love Story. The event consisted of five actors dressed in black, sitting on stools on a blank stage and reading from scripts they held before them like a book. I kept anticipating an outrageous one-liner, a flamboyantly gay character, or shocking sexuality. But instead—unlike the weird play Kenny had taken me to by the woman in his writing group—this was a simple story, a straight romance, with a plot that twisted here and there and characters I couldn't help but like.

One of the secondary characters, a writer, was a clear stand-in for Kenny. The guy had some terrific, smart-alecky lines. At one point in the second act, after a particularly apt bit of snark, the hero turned to the writer and shouted, "Hold up, Oscar Wilde. I'm not one of your characters."

I sat stunned. Sitting between my mother and my brother and hearing my words from the stage felt dangerous and sexy and strangely comforting, like a confidence whispered in a crowded room.

At the end of the second act the boy got the girl, and the audience applauded, some jumping to their feet, others stumbling up more reluctantly, but by the last bow, everyone was up and clapping. I looked down at my mother, who was pressing a tissue to one eye and then the other.

She smiled up at me. "What a sweet story. I'd like to meet your friend and tell him how much I enjoyed the show."

I quit breathing.

Cheryl grabbed my elbow. "Let's go get Kenny and bring him out to say hello." As we walked backstage she whispered, "Don't worry. It'll be okay."

I stared at her. "What are you talking about?"

Cheryl shook her head. "Forget it. Look. There he is."

I hadn't seen Kenny in a week and was surprised by how happy it made me to see him. My first thought was that he looked gorgeous. My second was that with all that product in his hair even my mother would know he was gay. I told myself it didn't matter. All sorts of people had gay friends. Especially in LA.

"Kenny, that was wonderful," Cheryl gushed as we got closer.

"Did you like it?" He was staring at me.

"Yes." I wanted to touch him, but that was insane. I stuck my hands in my pockets. "I recognized a few lines."

He grinned. "I hope you don't mind that I appropriated them."

I smiled back. "At least you gave them to the dashing young man, not the old colonel."

Cheryl cleared her throat. "Don't look now, but here comes your family, George."

I turned to see my mother, brother, and niece approaching, all three with expectant, wholesome Midwestern smiles on their faces.

Kenny winked. "Don't worry. I'll be good."

I tried not to sound nervous as I spoke to my family. "Hey, everyone. This is Kenny Marks, the playwright."

He held out his hand to my mother. "I'm so pleased to meet you, Mrs. Zajac."

She held his hand and smiled up into his face. "Please call me Debbie. What a sweet play you've written."

Al slapped Kenny on the shoulder. "It was great, just great. We're on our way to dinner. Do you want to come?"

"I don't know if Kenny…" I started.

Kenny glanced at me. His smile faltered. "Thanks. I'd love to. But I really can't tonight." Which was the right thing, the safe thing, for him to say.

So why did I feel like such an ass?

2006: An October Wedding

I opened the bottle of white Bordeaux, a subtle vintage that I used to buy regularly back when I was a successful broker and flew first class. I still had a chunk of money—the proceeds from my partner, Anne's new husband, buying me out. I'd chosen to leave it in the market, slowly building and ready for my next adventure. Which meant it was rare that I bought a fifty-dollar bottle of wine. But when Kenny told me he'd finished his latest screenplay, I wanted to splurge and treat him. I was refilling his glass when the phone rang.

I checked the caller ID. "David?"

Kenny's eyebrows flew up. "Only-gay-friend David?"

Listening to David's voice I realized I missed having a simple friendship.

Kenny watched me over his wineglass. "And here I thought he was an imaginary gay friend."

I stepped inside, leaving Kenny and his sarcasm on the balcony. David sounded good, much less shaky than the newly sober kid I'd befriended my first day in cooking school. During our years in school he'd bloomed, and now it seemed he was in an even better place than when I'd left New York. As we talked I pictured him the way I'd last seen him—barrel-chested and healthy, his shaved head gleaming in the sun. By the time I hung up the phone, I was grinning.

I sat across from Kenny and sipped my wine, which was silky on my tongue. "Not only is he not imaginary, he'll be here next week."

"Here, here?" Kenny gestured to the apartment.

I nodded. "He's moving back home to Portland from New York and decided to take the scenic route, stopping to visit a friend in Arizona and passing through Los Angeles on his way."

"That's quite a detour." Kenny swirled his wine.

"I guess." I watched the wine's legs bleed down his glass.

Kenny was quiet for a long time. He threw back the last of his wine and cocked his head at me. "Shall we adjourn to the other room?"

As always, a bolt of excitement shot through me at the thought of touching Kenny. I didn't understand how he could make me feel hot and safe at the same time. Maybe because he knew what I needed and he never failed to give it to me. I drained my glass and followed him inside, where I forgot all about David as Kenny held my head and fucked my mouth.

As we were falling asleep, Kenny nudged me. "We're having a party next week at my house. A couple of friends are having a commitment ceremony. They registered last month as domestic partners to take advantage of the new laws, and now they want to formalize it. They're calling it their like-a-wedding-but-not party. A few of the local chefs are donating food. I thought maybe you could put that doughnut fryer to work for a different good cause."

"Sure, I'll make doughnuts. But I don't want to go to a party." He had to know that by now.

Kenny gave me an exasperated look. "Maybe the elusive imaginary gay best friend could go. Or is he too closeted to have a good time too?"

If Kenny had to go with someone, it might as well be David. "I'll ask."

* * * *

David's visit coincided with two full dark days on the events calendar. Kenny swore he was locking himself in to work on his latest project, although he showed up for a few hours David's first night looking handsome and charming, purportedly amazed by David's actual existence.

When he left, David gave me an apologetic look. "I could stay at a hotel if you want."

I shook my head. "You're fine. Kenny and I are just friends."

David frowned. "That's not the vibe I got."

I shrugged. "Friends with benefits."

"That sounds dangerous." David's gaze was kind. "Someone's bound to fall in love."

I walked toward the kitchen, determined to move away from his concern. "That's not an option."

"He's involved with someone else?"

I shook my head.

"You're involved with someone else?"

I grabbed a box of crackers and ripped off the plastic. "He deserves better, okay? I don't want to talk about it." I dumped crackers onto a plate.

I hadn't meant to snap. I could feel him watching me.

David started arranging the crackers. "You're a nice guy, George. He could do a lot worse."

I wasn't about to talk with David about all the reasons I'd make a spectacularly bad boyfriend. After a while I nodded toward my doughnut fryer. "You want to make doughnuts tomorrow? I've been giving them away to the neighborhood homeless on my days off. We could make enough for the party and still have some to give away."

David looked at the fryer, gleaming in stainless steel glory in the corner of my kitchen area. "Isn't that sort of Marie Antoinette? Let them eat cake."

I shook my head. "I'm not royalty. I can't solve poverty. All I can do is give people the occasional treat."

"What do you do? Hand them out every Tuesday or something?"

"No." I put a hunk of cheese on the plate, in the center of the sunburst of crackers that David had arranged. "It's not a set day. I don't want people expecting too much." I carried the plate toward the balcony.

David followed. He sat across from me. "Sounds a bit like what you're doing in your relationship."

"I don't have a relationship." I watched a car pass on the street below, same make as Kenny's, only red.

"Right." David propped his feet on the railing.

I changed the subject.

* * * *

David went to Kenny's party. He didn't come home. I spent the night staring at the ceiling, imagining the two of them naked and trying to ignore the twisting of my gut.

When David got home at about two the next afternoon, he was grinning like a kid and talking about this handsome chef he'd met the night before. Relief washed through me, followed by shame. I'd been saying that Kenny deserved better, and it didn't get better than David Schwartz. So why hadn't I been happy thinking of the two of them together? I realized with a sinking feeling that it was because while Kenny could definitely do better than me, I wouldn't ever find anyone better than him. Since I didn't intend to inflict myself on him permanently, that was a depressing thought.

* * * *

"He's bad news." Kenny accelerated onto the freeway.

We were on our way to the valley for an intimate gathering of one hundred of a bride's closest friends. In Iowa, bridal showers were organized to help the new bride set up her kitchen. For L'Ouest clients, they seemed to be opportunities to show off that the bride didn't need toasters or blenders because she could hire someone else to cook.

"Who's bad news?" I leaned back in my seat and watched the traffic.

"Rick, the guy your David went home with."

"David seemed to like him."

Kenny looked uncomfortable. "Rick's not exactly a catch, but I was relieved. I wasn't sure exactly what kind of friends were you with David. Then I figured if he was going home with Rick, maybe he hadn't been getting much lately."

I looked at him.

"Rick appeals to a man's mothering instincts. Come to think of it, so do you." He focused on the road. "You'd tell me if you slept with anyone else, right? I mean, that's our deal."

"Of course." I smiled. "I only have one bed, so technically I slept with David. But we stayed on our own sides of the bed, if that's what you're asking. Why would you think I had sex with David? We're just friends."

Kenny cut his eyes at me. "So are we. Or that's what you keep telling me."

He had a point. "David's the marrying type. I don't think he'd do casual."

Kenny didn't say anything.

I knew I should keep my mouth shut, but I wasn't good at that. "I mean, he's sweet. Kind of innocent. I don't think he could handle my...you know."

"Good for him." Kenny shook his head. "I hadn't expected him to be so young and hot."

We drove in silence for a while.

"Obviously you think of me as jaded, slutty, and fickle," Kenny muttered as we turned into the bride's driveway.

"What?" I gaped at him. Kenny was great. He had to know I thought that by now.

"Nothing." He slammed the van into park.

The bride was striding across her lawn toward us, so I let it go.

* * * *

I'd been feeling it for weeks, ever since David left. Kenny wasn't happy with our sex life. It was definitely taking me longer to get him off. But he kept coming over. I tried to ignore his disappointment and prayed he wouldn't find anyone soon.

It came to a head late one night. We'd gotten off work and had to be back early the next morning, so I'd asked Kenny to stay over. It had taken far too long for him to say yes.

We dropped our clothes and climbed into bed. I flipped off the light and waited—horny—for Kenny to have his way with me. He lay there staring into the darkness.

I touched his arm. "So do you want—"

He turned on his side, cradling his head in his hands. "I'm not sure I can get what I want, George."

Fear settled into my belly. "What do you want?"

"Something different." He flopped onto his back. "It's like we're stuck in this ritualized dance. I'm not this major top, and even if I was, this wouldn't—"

"I thought you liked what we were doing."

He waved his hands in the air like he was dispersing a bad smell. "I did. I do. But it's so limited. And there's a long list of things you won't do." He ticked them off on his fingers. "You don't initiate, won't sixty-nine, don't want me to fuck you, and the rules are that I have to force you to do anything. I'm starting to feel like an asshole." He turned again and held my eye. "I know we're just friends, but can't we ever do tender?"

The fear was creeping through my body. My nose filled with the smell of cow shit. I whispered, "Are you ordering me to be tender?"

"No." It came out of him like an explosion. I started to shake.

Kenny whispered, "Oh, shit. Baby, you're shaking."

I was trembling all over. It was humiliating and horrifying. I willed myself to stop. It only got worse.

Kenny wrapped me in his arms. "Shhh, it's okay."

Even though I was shaking so hard I could barely control my hand, I reached for his cock. I ought to be man enough to do this.

Kenny took my hand and held it to his chest. "Let's go to sleep. We're both tired."

And as if his words were a magical incantation, the fear receded, and my shivering slowed. Exhaustion swept over me.

As I was drifting off, Kenny whispered, "That's not a kink, honey. It's a sickness. Maybe you should see someone, like a therapist."

When we woke in the morning, neither of us spoke of the night before. I kept waiting for him to bring it up as wave after wave of mortification swept over me. But he didn't.

He took the next few nights off to write. When he returned to my bed, we went on as if nothing had happened. Except, of course, it had.

2007: A February Wedding

"It's sort of like a costume party." Kenny was explaining the Purim party to Cheryl. "The temple I grew up in had it mostly as a kid thing—a Purim carnival with costumes and games and crap like that. Sort of Halloween in early spring. But it's the perfect grown-up holiday. You're supposed to drink until you can't tell the difference between right and wrong."

One of the busboys yelled, "Sounds like my kind of holiday."

Kenny passed out brightly colored cards. "It's a week from tomorrow night at a bar downtown. I have invitations for everyone. You have to come in costume."

His smile was tentative as he handed me a card. I stuffed it in my pocket. The only way I'd been to the bars was late at night after everyone was drunk and wouldn't remember who they picked up. Kenny's party sounded more public than that.

I'd made Stephan call in as many helpers as possible since we had three weddings scheduled for Valentine's weekend, two with heavy appetizers and one sit-down. Given we could only use the kitchen in the mornings before the regular crew arrived, it would take us most of a week to get ready, and that with waiters and bussers helping with prep.

I had Kenny playing gofer while the busboys washed vegetables and prep cooks sliced, diced, and made merry.

"What are you going as?" Cheryl didn't look up from the petit fours she was decorating.

Kenny picked up a platter of cold cuts and pirouetted twice on his way to the walk-in cooler. "Queen Esther, of course. Who else?"

My hand jerked, and I messed up a mustard rose on the platter I'd been preparing. "Shit."

Kenny narrowed his eyes at me. "You should come as Mordecai, Queen Esther's beneficent uncle and pimp."

"Pimp?" Cheryl stopped what she was doing. "I thought this was a religious holiday."

"It is. It's all in the Book of Esther—the whole megillah." He giggled. "Esther's uncle Mordecai sends her to the king for a night of queen tryouts, sort of like The Bachelor, only all the contestants start the night as virgins. Esther gets the job."

Cheryl snorted. "I don't even remember when I was a virgin."

I traded Kenny a full platter for an empty one. "I'm not going."

Kenny stared at me. The kitchen went silent.

Kenny of all people ought to have known there was no way I was going to a party where men dressed up as Queen Esther. I couldn't believe he would expect me to expose myself like that.

I could feel everyone watching me. "What? I don't like costume parties."

"You're not coming to the party?" Kenny asked.

Cheryl gave a disgusted shake of her head.

"You don't need me. I'm sure there are plenty of other people who like that sort of thing." God, I sounded like my dad. What a shitty thought. But I was not going anywhere with Kenny on a night when people drank enough that they couldn't tell the difference between right and wrong. God knew what I'd do or say.

"I'm sure there are." Kenny took the tray and walked back to the cooler.

"Sometimes you're an asshole," Cheryl whispered.

We're not a couple, I wanted to say to shut her up. Instead I concentrated on making perfect mustard flowers. It wasn't my fault he'd gotten hurt. I'd been honest from the beginning about what I could and couldn't do. What did he expect?

* * * *

Valentine's Day weekend slammed into us. I could barely catch my breath. The hours were crazy, and both nights I fell into bed alone only to have to scramble out a few hours later to start the next sixteen-hour sprint. At one point I swore that if I saw another sappy pink heart, I'd puke. Kenny seemed distant. But hell, we were all snapping at each other. Especially when the wedding photographer for the first wedding stopped by the restaurant and ended up taking pictures of the wrong cake, which slowed everything down by an hour we didn't have.

By Sunday night I was so beat that I didn't give it a second thought when Kenny said he'd rather go back to his own apartment.

But on Monday, when he didn't answer my phone call, I began to get angry.

"Is this about the party?" I asked on my second phone message. "You're being childish."

The third time I hung up before the beep. He'd have to talk to me the next night at work. I hoped.

* * * *

Weeknights tended to be light. That Wednesday we had a corporate event requiring one waiter and a vanload of finger food. The budget wasn't big, so Cheryl prepped and I assembled. Stephan had instructed us that if we managed to get finished in time, he'd let us leave the dishes for regular crew. The implied threat was that if we dawdled, the two of us would be stuck on KP duty, which wasn't in either of our contracts.

Cheryl passed me a bowl of sliced tomatoes and started on the onions. "You are going to Kenny's party tomorrow, right?"

"I already said I'm not going."

"But you didn't mean it, did you? I mean, he's inviting all his theater friends. He'll want them to meet you."

I tried to keep my voice level as I asked, "And why would Kenny want his friends to meet me?"

"Aren't you…" She paused. "I guess I just assumed…" When I didn't answer, she shrugged. "None of my business. You want more of these, or should I start on the pastry dough?"

We had everything prepped by the time Kenny arrived to help load the van. The plan was to drive the food over and unload, have the secretary in charge give Kenny his instructions, and then we'd have a couple hours off before the event began. Assuming Kenny was over his little snit, I had a few plans for how I wanted to spend that extra time.

But Kenny was subdued. He nodded toward a tray of savory pastries. "You want those on the lower rack?"

Cheryl looked from one to the other of us. She picked up the tray. "I'll get these." She practically trotted out of the kitchen.

Kenny leaned down to pick up another tray. I stopped him, my hand on his arm. "What's wrong?"

He gave a disgusted sniff, and shook his head.

I grabbed his other arm and pulled him to face me. He turned away. "Why are you stonewalling me like this? What did I do?"

He looked back at me slowly, his arms limp beneath my hands. "Stonewalling? That's nice coming from you."

"Is this about the goddamned party?" I shook his arm. "I don't like parties. I don't like being on display."

He pulled away and turned back to the trays. "No. It's not about the party, or not just about the party. Drop it, okay?"

I grabbed his shoulder and spun him back to face me. "No, I don't want to drop it. I thought we were friends."

He winced like he was in pain. "Friends. Always fucking friends. We're not friends, George. We're lovers. Whether you like it or not, that's what we are, or at least what we have been."

I felt like he'd hit me. I stood staring at him. "But we said—"

"No, you said." His shoulders sagged. "I can't do it anymore, George. I'm tired of feeling like your shameful secret."

"I'm not…" But I couldn't say it, because he was right. I didn't want to be seen in public with him. But I didn't want to stop seeing him in private either.

"I know." Kenny took my face in his hands. "You're almost forty, George. When are you going to figure out that no one important really cares who you sleep with?"

I only want you. That's all I could think as I stared into his eyes. I leaned forward to kiss him, and he let me, a long, tender touch of lips and tongues that felt disconcertingly like good-bye.

A door slammed, and suddenly Stephan's voice was booming through the kitchen. "What the fuck is going on?"

Kenny and I flew apart.

Kenny muttered, "Shit," as he turned toward the noise.

I whirled to face Stephan. He was bearing down on us, his face a red balloon of disapproval.

"I can explain…" I started, not sure what I'd say next but feeling like I had to protect Kenny. I think I may even have stepped in front of Kenny as if that would shield him from whatever was coming next.

"You can explain why you're kissing a waiter?" Stephan planted himself inches from me. "And not even a pretty one. You disgust me. You're fired."

"But—"

Kenny's hand on my shoulder stopped me. "It was my fault, Stephan. Fire me."

"No." I shook my head. "I'm the one who should be fired. Kenny did nothing wrong."

Stephan stared at us, one hand on his hip and a sneer on his face. "How sweet. You're both fired. Now get out of here. If you see that woman, Cheryl, send her down here. She's about to get the job she always wanted." He glared at me. "Yours."

I stayed to argue. It didn't change anything, and by the time I got to the staff room to clean out my locker, Kenny was already gone.

* * * *

I didn't read the label on my second bottle of wine. It didn't fucking matter. Wrapping myself in a blanket against the cool night air, I sat on the balcony and watched the neighborhood. A couple was having a fight somewhere down the block, a real knock-down-drag-out. Three different kinds of music competed for my early-evening attention. I could hear the traffic on the boulevard two streets over.

Maybe I should go back to New York. Except I didn't have a job there either, just an angry ex-wife, some confused ex-colleagues, and a bunch of ex-one-night stands. An ex-life, that's what I had in New York. And it was beginning to look the same in Los Angeles, with my ex-job and my ex…friend, fuck buddy, what? Kenny was wrong. We weren't lovers. I couldn't be anyone's lover. I'd never promised him anything. Never. I was clear as glass from day one. Clear as fucking glass.

I drained my glass and poured another. It was my fault Stephan fired us. I had to make it up to Kenny somehow. Because Kenny didn't deserve to lose his job over something as inconsequential as a kiss. Although kissing Kenny never felt inconsequential. It was hot and tender and... I had to fix this. Fix the job and fix the friendship. I could crawl on my belly back to Stephan. The thought made me sick to my stomach. I'd do it for Kenny, though. I would.

A panel truck chugged along on the street below. Wouldn't something that size be better than the fucking van? You could probably fit a whole kitchen in that thing. I paused with my glass halfway to my mouth. A kitchen in a truck. What a fantastic idea.

I jumped up. The edge of the blanket caught the table and jostled it, sending my half-full second bottle of wine crashing to the concrete floor of the balcony. Fuck it. I'd deal with that later. I dropped the blanket over the pool of wine and broken glass. I thumbed Kenny's number into my phone. He didn't pick up. I'd talk to him in the morning. First I needed to figure out how much a panel truck cost and where I could get it outfitted and how to get licenses and inspections and...

I dropped onto my bed and flipped open my laptop. Everything a person might want to know was on the Internet, right?

* * * *

I checked the address, wondering how it was that in all the time I'd known Kenny, I'd never been to his house. It turned out to be a large two-story Mission-style with a small rock garden in front. I ran a hand through my hair, ruffling it after the bike ride over. It was after noon, and the air smelled of eucalyptus. The day didn't seem warm enough for the amount I was sweating.

The mat in front of the door spelled out WELCOME in bright red letters. I wondered if that was true. After last night, Kenny still wasn't accepting my phone calls. But he'd have to be pleased with my news.

I took a deep breath and pushed the doorbell. Moments later I could hear footsteps. They stopped at the door. There was a long pause.

"Kenny?" I put my hand on the door, as if to placate him. "Let me in. I need to talk with you."

Pause.

A lock clicked, and the door swung open. Kenny stood there in sweatpants and an old T-shirt. Even scowling he looked beautiful.

He leaned against the doorway, arms crossed. "We're not leaving for the party until eight."

"I'm not here for the party."

"Right. That's what you said. No party for George."

I shifted my weight. "Please, can I come in? I have something important to talk with you about."

His eyes held mine for a moment. He launched himself off the door frame and walked back into the house.

I followed, closing the door behind me.

Kenny led me into a brightly lit kitchen, where three men sat around a table strewn with poster-making supplies. One was filling in the letters for a banner that read Let's hear it for the Queens.

"This is George," Kenny said as we entered.

The men stopped what they were doing and stared at me.

A man wearing thick black eyeliner jumped up. "All right, girls," he said, with the emphasis on the last syllable. "Let's take this party to the living room and give them some privacy."

They dispersed, glancing furtively at me. I felt thoroughly exposed and wondered how much detail about us Kenny had shared.

I watched their retreating backs. "Your roommates?"

He shook his head. "They're all at work. These are a few friends who came over to help me get ready for the party and to console…" He sat on one of the vacated stools and gestured toward another for me. "So what did you want to talk about?"

"I've had the best idea." I leaned across the table, willing him to get as excited about it as I was. "I'm going to start my own catering company. I've got a line on a panel truck, and I'm getting bids for the remodel. It'll be great, Kenny. We've already got the contacts. I know Libby will throw us some business and—"

He held up his hand. "We?"

I smiled. "That's the best part. You can come work for me, and I'll see if I can get Cheryl—"

He stopped me again. "You've come to offer me a job?"

I nodded. "It's my fault that Stephan fired you and—"

"No, thank you." Kenny stared at me incredulously.

I tried again. "You can't still be pissed about the party. If it means that much to you—"

Kenny closed his eyes. I stopped talking.

He took a deep breath and opened his eyes. "You still don't get it, do you? George, it's not about the party, and it's not about Stephan. I'm glad you're starting your own company. Congratulations. You'll be good at it."

"So come work with me." I could hear the whine in my voice.

He shrugged. "I'll get something soon. There are always jobs waiting tables."

"But this would be more than that. This would be an adventure." I pulled the business plan I'd roughed out over coffee out of my back pocket. "Look. With reasonable projections, within a year we'll break even, and two tops for profitability."

He didn't look at the paper I thrust toward him. "And how am I supposed to pay the rent until then?"

"I've got money saved. I'll pay you a salary and—"

"No." Kenny shuddered. "I can't believe you even would suggest that."

"What?" The implication hit me. How could he think I would ask him to… "No, I wouldn't pay you for sex. We'd be working together. Although—"

Kenny stood, his stool crashing to the floor. "No! No. No, I'll find a job. Don't worry about that."

I stared at him. I'd never seen Kenny this upset. He turned his back to me.

I whispered, "What do you want?"

His shoulders dropped. I barely heard his answer. "You can't give me what I want."

I crossed the room, grabbed him by the shoulder, and spun him around. "Kenny, I never promised that."

He nodded, his eyes focused on the middle of my chest. "I know. And maybe it's unfair of me to want it, but I do. It hurts too much to be with you the way we've been. I can't do that anymore."

I stroked his arms. "We can stop. Work together as friends, if you want. Just friends, no benefits."

His dark eyes were pools of pain as they met mine. "I can't do that. And I don't think you can either."

Hoping to stop the avalanche I could feel coming, I tried for humor. "You're sexy, but you're not that—"

"I love you." He said it simply, like he was talking about the weather. "And you love me. I know you do. But whatever twisted-up, closeted thing you've got going won't let you see it."

Kenny stepped out of my grasp and walked back to the counter. He picked up an empty balloon and began playing with it. I stood stock-still, watching him. I felt numb and couldn't get my thoughts to organize themselves into a cohesive sentence.

Kenny broke the silence. "No one cares that you're gay. You should know that, George."

"Oh, I think my mother would care. My father sure would have."

"Your father is dead." He looked up at me, his face angry for the first time. "Your mother would get over it. I'm sure my mother would have rather I married some nice Jewish girl and given her lots of grandbabies. But she got over it. She cried for two weeks after I came out. Now she's past president of her local PFLAG chapter. She's your mother. She'll deal."

"You don't understand." The smell, the feel of the barn was heavy on me.

"No, you don't understand. You're almost forty years old. Don't you think it's time you grew a pair?"

I stepped forward, my fists balled. "Fuck you."

He held my gaze until I relaxed my fists, if not my jaw.

"I'm sorry. That was uncalled for." Kenny turned away. "You should go."

I moved forward. At the doorway I turned and said, "If you change your mind about the job, call me."

He nodded. I walked down the hallway and opened the front door.

Kenny followed me. "Get some help, George."

The door shut behind me. I stood blinking in the bright California sun, leaving Kenny to his gay buddies, his gay life, and his gay-loving mother.

"You love me." Of course I loved Kenny. Who wouldn't? But it was better this way. Now he'd be free to find someone decent and leave the walking wounded behind. I slid my helmet on before anyone could see me cry.

IOWA

2008: A June Wedding

Out the window, the landscape looked like a patchwork quilt. Iowa—home of corn, pigs, and my unhappy childhood—spread beneath me in squares of green and brown, cut through by straight roads and twisting rivers. I took a long sip of my five-dollar glass of bad airplane wine. It wasn't enough to quell my free-floating anxiety. The last time I'd landed in Des Moines, we were burying my father. This time we were marrying off his granddaughter.

"This might be a good time to think about why you feel the need to be forced into the sexual acts you enjoy." Only one of the assignments Dr. Bernstein had given me for the weekend. The easy one. The other—coming out—was a terrifying prospect. I had no idea if I'd grown the balls I would need to carry it out.

The seat belt sign dinged. Here we go. Another Zajac family event.

Jessica met me in the terminal, throwing her arms around me in a hug that went some way to calming my anxiety. "Dad's in the car. Thanks for coming, Uncle George. It means a lot."

I looped my arm around her shoulder and let her lead me toward the baggage carousel. "Are you kidding? Of all the weddings I've been to this year—and believe me, I've been to my share—this is the only one worth seeing."

She giggled. "You won't say that when you hear that we're putting you to work. Grandma's insisting that everything be homemade, but with her arthritis—"

"My pierogi skills are rusty, but I'll do what I can."

Out at the curb, Al was waiting, standing beside a shiny sedan with dealer plates. His smile widened when he saw me. As he pulled me into a bear hug, I started to relax. It might not be so bad being home.

Jessica and Al kept up a nonstop discussion of the wedding as we headed east and then north, past the suburbs of Des Moines and out onto the flatlands of home. We passed verdant cornfields spiked with wind turbines. The car flew along straight roads for an hour. With nothing to break the view from horizon to horizon, the sun beat even brighter than at home in Los Angeles. As always, the landscape made me feel small and sad. Dr. Bernstein would say that was projection, but what did she know? This was the world in which my father had raged like the storms that swept across the land, drenching the earth. After a storm, there might be a rainbow. After one of my father's fits, there never was.

When my father died, Mom quit farming. She sold the fields to a neighbor. I'd heard that she knocked down the barn, but it was a shock to see the white farmhouse standing alone with its single wide oak tree and swath of manicured lawn stretching over the footprint of the old barn. Six years before, when I'd been home for the funeral, a sharp January wind had blown whirlwinds of snow across the fields and piled drifts against the barn wall.

Everything looked different on a sunny June day. The house seemed larger out of the shadow of the barn. It practically sparkled in the sunlight. She must have had it painted in anticipation of the wedding. As I stepped out of the car, I inhaled the smell of newly mowed grass.

The screen door opened and closed with a bang as Mom stepped out onto the porch, wiping her hands on the bright floral apron I'd sent her for Christmas. Did she look older than when I'd last seen her? I couldn't tell. But as she opened her arms to hug me, it was clear she was glad I came.

At least for now.

* * * *

"Wow, Mom. You've been busy." I looked around. Every counter in the old white kitchen was covered with chrusciki—pastry bow ties drenched in honey that took a lot longer to make than the doughnut holes I still cooked on days off.

"This is nothing. You should have seen when I got married. My mother cooked for days." She gestured toward

Al, who stood in the doorway watching us. "And we gave those two a good send-off. You, on the other hand, wanted none of the old ways."

I shrugged. "Anne and her mother organized the whole thing."

She shook her head. "It's bad luck to ignore tradition."

"Let's hope Jessica has better luck than we did." Al snagged a chrusciki, barely avoiding Mom's slap.

"What's he like?"

Al swallowed the pastry whole. "Tom? He's a nice guy. I think he'll be good for her. I wish they'd waited until they were both out of school with good jobs. As it is, they'll be eating a lot of ramen."

Mom waved her hand at him. "She's the same age you were when you got married. And two years older than I was."

A timer dinged, and Mom opened the oven door. A cloud of cinnamon-soaked steam rolled out as she pulled the sheets of pastries out and replaced them with dough-covered pans.

Al frowned. "Those first years were hard, though. Of course, as things turned out I wouldn't trade them for the world."

Mom turned to him, her hand on her hip. "Let's hope these two have enough sense to wait before they start having children."

Al winced. "Point taken. That was a long time ago."

Her face softened. "It was, and I'm thankful for every day that sweet girl was part of our family." She cut her eyes at me, reminding us all exactly what she'd thought of my own, somewhat snobby wife.

"Yes, I know. And Anne wasn't your dream daughter-in-law. Now how can I help?"

She nodded toward a bowl of apples. "Those need washing and slicing."

"That's my cue to go," Al announced. "I'm meeting Brother Howard at the church to talk about when we can pick up the tables and chairs."

Mom wrinkled her nose. "That man is a self-righteous pig." I looked at her sharply. Bad-mouthing church folk wasn't like her, although it didn't seem to faze Al.

Mom reached into the pocket of her apron and brought out a folded sheet of paper. "As long as you're going to town, you can stop and get a few things."

Al unfolded the paper. "I don't know if I can fit all this in my car."

She waved a dishcloth at him. "Go on, you, before I make you peel potatoes."

With a grin he ducked out the door.

The room felt too peaceful to ask her about Brother Howard. We worked in silence. It felt good to be in her kitchen again. All the happy moments of my childhood happened there—making Christmas rolls or Easter bread or chocolate-chip cookies on a Sunday afternoon. The linoleum was more scuffed and the cabinets needed paint, but it still smelled of cabbage and pot roast and love.

Mom was rolling out pie dough. She paused and looked at me. "Is it my fault? That your marriage didn't work out?"

My heartbeat raced. We were not going to have this conversation now. I was not going to steal Jessica's day. No coming out until after the wedding.

"Nothing's your fault, Mom."

She shook her head. "Your father used to get so mad at me for letting you play in the kitchen. He said I was making a girl out of you."

"Dad was angry about a lot of things." I kept my gaze on the apple I was scrubbing, afraid of what I'd see in her eyes, terrified that if I saw even a glimmer of understanding, I'd start babbling and ruin everything.

She sighed. "Sometimes I wonder…"

And yet I couldn't help hoping it could be that easy. I looked up when she trailed off. "What do you wonder?"

She focused again on rolling the dough. "He was a hard man."

She could say that again. I kept my mouth shut and started slicing. My knife slid through the white flesh like grace.

* * * *

Jessica brought her groom to dinner. With short curly hair, granny glasses, and a bow tie, Jessica's Tom looked like he'd stepped out of the past century. He was an earnest young man, but he gazed at Jessica with worshipful awe, and that was bound to warm an uncle's heart.

They were young. Freshly minted college graduates, about to start graduate school in the fall. As I watched them talk, I imagined them cuddling in an underheated studio apartment, propped on pillows, reading books, a bowl of microwave popcorn or instant noodles for dinner. A long way from my own unhappy newlywed days. Anne's father had gotten me my first job in finance, a high-powered gig where I was over my head and had to swim like hell to survive. She'd worked for a fashion magazine, and we'd lived in her parents' Manhattan apartment, attended her parents' social events, and I'd tried not to piss off the servants.

I couldn't imagine why I'd thought things would work out with Anne. As I sat at my mother's dinner table and listened to the simple conversation, it occurred to me that all my running away had been the twenty-something equivalent of a temper tantrum. Sure, I'd had it rough with my dad, and I'd wanted to be as far away from Iowa as possible, but this sitting and talking and eating mashed potatoes drenched in butter, maybe I hadn't needed to give that up.

And then Brother Howard showed up with a truckload of folding chairs, just in time for dessert. Mom scooped out giant portions of peach cobbler, stained sugar dripping from her spoon, and Jessica poured coffee—regular, no decaf here in the heartland.

Brother Howard was a fiftyish, dark-haired man whose belly overflowed his tan polyester pants. He was the deacon at New Pentecostal. We'd met at my sister-in-law's and my father's funerals. He hesitated before shaking my hand but, once committed, pumped with religious vigor and sat in the empty chair beside me.

"You'll be coming to church on Sunday," he boomed.

I glanced at my mother. "Actually, I thought I might stay here and take care of whatever last-minute details need doing."

"Hear the word of the Lord, you rulers of Sodom," he intoned solemnly.

I tried to keep my expression neutral. "I'm sure it will be a very nice service, but I'd like to help out here. After all, you could say I'm a wedding professional."

He sneered at me. "Always a bridesmaid, never a bride, eh?"

"Excuse me?" I stared at him.

My brother shifted in his chair. "This cobbler's good, Mom. You outdid yourself."

Jessica looked like she wanted to run out of the room, and Tom gaped open-mouthed as Brother Howard continued, "The ways of the flesh are sin, George. You've been living in the fleshpots of Sodom and Gomorrah too long."

My mother brandished her fork at him. "Oh, be quiet, Howard, and eat your cobbler. You're not here to save souls tonight. You're delivering furniture."

Howard looked like he might speak again, but a glare from my mother shut him up.

I bit into my cobbler, too sweet and a little overcooked. Mom hadn't changed her recipe in all these years, but clearly some other things had changed. Where had this fiery woman been when my father was alive?

* * * *

The day of the wedding, there wasn't a cloud in the deep blue sky. When the others left for church, I drank another cup of bad coffee and wandered barefoot into the backyard to make sure everything was ready for the afternoon. The banners we'd strung the night before fluttered in the breeze. Dew pooled on the seats of the metal folding chairs. The sun would surely dry them out before the guests arrived.

With the barn gone it seemed you could see for miles. There was a metaphor for Dr. Bernstein. I gazed out at the growing corn. I'd hated it growing up, those vast expanses of waving plants. Now, after years in New York and Los Angeles, it seemed foreign, like a lunar landscape.

I wondered what Kenny would think of this terrain. It was funny how often I missed him. Dr. Bernstein thought I should look him up. But Cheryl said he was involved with someone, a doctor, someone who gave him what he needed, a public relationship—a life in the sun. And it was only right. He was so funny, so gorgeous, so kind. How could he still be single? And I didn't want to face the fact that I'd thrown him away. Instead I stood in my mother's backyard in Iowa, staring down memories and imagining him there, lounging in the grass, one leg draped elegantly over the other, smiling up at me from beneath spiky blond hair.

Dr. Bernstein said I'd never meet anyone else if I kept dreaming of Kenny as the guy who got away. But I knew confronting him wouldn't fix that. Because she was right. I'd never find anyone else like him.

A few steps and I was standing in the ghost footprint of the old barn. The lawn here looked the same as the rest, but beneath my feet it felt haunted, whether by my father or the memory of my fear, I couldn't say. I paced the periphery of where I remembered the barn standing. The grass was cool, and I inhaled the fresh green scent of an Iowa spring. My mother had planted pink roses in the far corner, the spot where my father had set up his "educational" area, what Dr. Bernstein called his torture chamber. I held a rose to my nose and breathed in the sweetness. I watched honeybees leap among the flowers, their fat bodies yellow with pollen.

"Why do you need to be forced?"

I had a sudden image of myself standing in the barn, naked, my adolescent cock betraying me. "It's not my fault, Daddy. It's not my fault."

I sank to the ground and put my head in my hands. It's not my fault. I felt sick to my stomach with the realization of how my father haunted even the most private desires. Alone, sitting on the grass in the graveyard of my youth, I cried, rocking back and forth as alternating waves of sorrow and anger washed through me. I poured it all into the ground, which had soaked up so many of my tears before.

When the waves passed, I lay back and looked up at the sky. It didn't matter how long it took me; I would learn a different way of loving. Because I wanted that, wanted to feel whole and loved, to love someone. No, not someone— to love a man, with my whole heart and body.

Kenny'd been right. It wasn't a kink. It was a wound, and wounds heal.

I stood, brushed off the grass as best I could, and walked back toward the house. I straightened my shoulders. I had a life to live, a real life. Not to mention there was wedding food to prepare.

* * * *

The planned ceremony was beautiful, a mix of old and new. Before the ceremony, Al called me to join Mom, Tom, and his mousy parents in the living room.

Al looked splendid in a dark suit cut to emphasize his shoulders and hide his aging high-school-linebacker paunch. Mom wore a peach chiffon dress that brought out the glow in her cheeks. Tom still looked like a frontier store clerk who'd for some reason put on a tux. His parents wore brown and seemed to fade in with the woodwork.

The six of us watched Jessica descend the stairs. Her dress couldn't have cost what the brides wore in Hollywood, and the local hair salon was no boutique, but she was the prettiest bride I'd seen all year. Tom appeared riveted by her approach.

Al blushed as he cleared his throat. "I know you're not interested in most of the old Polish traditions, but thank you for letting me do this."

Jessica took Tom's hand, and together they smiled at Al.

"My parents blessed me, and theirs blessed them." Al glanced sideways at me. "My brother decided to skip it, and look where that got him."

I snorted. "I knew there was an explanation."

Al shrugged. "Maybe not, but why turn down a blessing?" He focused on the young couple in front of him.

I held the tray while Al handed Jessica and Tom each a chunk of salted bread. "Bread so you'll never be hungry, salt to overcome the bitterness of life." They popped it in their mouths and chewed homemade bread, my contribution to the event. Mom wiped her eyes.

Al distributed the glasses of wine, one to each of us. He held up his. "And may you never be thirsty. To my beautiful Jessica and her husband Tom."

"To Jessica and Tom," we echoed and sipped the wine.

Al winked at Tom. "You're not going to be thirsty tonight. This is a Polish wedding."

Mom set her wineglass down on the tray with a shake of her head. "This is nothing like it was in my day. Oh, what parties those were. Days of dancing."

"And nights of yelling," I added. "Let's get this show on the road."

* * * *

The warm afternoon graded into a spring evening, with sweet-smelling breezes and bullfrogs that almost outsang the band.

My mother complained about the lack of a polka band. "What's a Polish wedding without polka?"

I liked the pickup folk rock music played by a group of Jessica and Tom's college friends. They managed to muddle through a handful of songs for each generation, making up in enthusiasm and good cheer what they lacked in proficiency.

They were stumbling through "Rock Around the Clock" when it was my turn to dance with Jessica.

"Not like the weddings you're used to, Uncle George."

"It's better. Weddings should be about family and love." I spotted Tom across the lawn dancing with one of the church ladies. "He seems like a nice guy."

She grinned. "He is."

The band hit a particularly sour note. Jessica winced.

I smiled at her. "Hey, at least they're free."

I spun her in a circle that made her laugh. When she twirled back into my arms, she asked shyly, "How about you, Uncle George? Anyone special?"

"Nope."

She leaned in and lowered her voice so that I could barely hear her over the music. "I want you to know that it doesn't matter, not to me or to Tom. I mean, whoever it is, it's okay with us."

I squeezed her close, wondering if Jessica realized what she was saying. "Thanks, Jessica. You're sweet. There isn't anyone. But if there ever is, I'll keep that in mind." For all I knew she was offering me permission to hook up with a woman of color or an atheist, but probably not a Jewish man.

Someone tapped me on the shoulder. I turned to see Brother Howard. My niece gave a wan smile and nodded, so I turned her over to the force of darkness. I didn't ask him if dancing was a sin. But I wanted to. I wandered over to the refreshment table, where Al slapped me on the back and pressed a shot of vodka into my palm. It seemed like just the thing.

A hundred strings of tiny white Christmas lights lit the backyard. It may not have been a true old-fashioned Polish wedding, but the party was definitely underway. Even Tom's parents seemed to have loosened up, probably with the help of a few of those vodka shots my brother was passing around. The band started a set of off-key torch songs. I leaned against the side of the house and gazed out at the swaying crowd. The guests wore their best big-box store clothing, the band played badly, and our citronella candles didn't quite keep all the mosquitoes away. In all the years I'd been catering LA weddings, there hadn't been one that touched my heart like this. Jessica and Tom looked so very young and happy, and I truly wished them well.

My mother approached on wobbly legs. She held a wineglass full of pale pink liquid that sloshed onto her good dress.

I caught her as she tripped. "Hey, Mom. Let's find a seat."

Taking her glass, I led her to a folding chair and held it as she fell onto the seat.

She patted my arm in a random drunken pattern. "You're a good boy, George."

I sat in the chair beside hers. "I don't know about that, Mom."

"You are." She looked at me with earnest, inebriated eyes. "What he did to you... It wasn't right."

I felt my eyes tearing. I'd had too much to drink, and so had she. This was not the time. "I'm sure he did what he thought was best."

She was shaking her head so vigorously I was afraid she might make herself sick. "I should have stopped him.

You were just a boy." And then she was crying, big blubbering tears.

I put my arm around her and pulled her close, wiping my eyes with my other hand. I brought out the silly handkerchief my brother had stuffed in the breast pocket of my suit and handed it to her. She blew her nose noisily.

I stroked her back. "It's okay, Mom. Don't cry."

She straightened and started wiping at her eyes, which had taken on the same hue as her bright red lipstick.

Again, she focused blearily on me. "That Kenny of yours seemed like a nice man."

"Kenny?" My voice sounded very small in my ears. I couldn't believe we were having this conversation.

She blew her nose again. "I want you to be happy, George. Your father was wrong. Life is too short to be unhappy."

I stared at her.

She patted my leg. "I think you should help me up to bed, dear. I don't feel well."

As I led her up the front steps, she turned to survey the party one last time. She was smiling when she looked up at me. "I love a good wedding."

"This is a good one, Mom. You did good."

I walked her upstairs and let her crumple onto her bed, took off her shoes, and covered her with a blanket.

I walked back downstairs and sat in the old living room, staring into the dark and thinking about love and life and forgiveness.

* * * *

They must have known what a drunken brawl the wedding would be, because Jessica and Tom had decided ahead of time to spend their first night of wedded bliss in the spare room at my mom's house. Most of the guests appeared to have gone home, although three members of the band were still asleep on the floor of the living room when I came down.

My mother sat at the kitchen table drinking coffee. She looked up when I walked in, waved, and settled back into her hangover. I remembered this from Al's wedding, the late-night drinking and the morning-after quiet. I poured myself coffee and set about making brunch for whoever showed up.

* * * *

After a few mimosas everyone perked up. It was late afternoon before all the guests left. Jessica and Tom went first, rattling off in Al's wedding present to them—a new Suburban decorated with tin cans and shaving-cream good wishes. Their first stop was to be a good-bye lunch at the hotel where Tom's parents were staying. Then they were off to the Boundary Waters wilderness for a weeklong honeymoon.

Once they were gone, the other young people who'd spent the night straggled out, leaving Mom and Al and me to clean up the backyard and put the house back together. Brother Howard showed up in the afternoon to help load chairs and tables onto his truck, and by sundown everything was normal in the farmhouse.

Mom rested a hand on Al's arm. "Stay to dinner. There are enough leftovers to feed the neighborhood."

"I'll help." I moved toward the kitchen, but she stopped me.

"You relax. I can find my way around my own kitchen."

Al and I stood in the living room watching her leave. I took a deep breath. Okay, Dr. Bernstein. It's judgment day.

Al poured scotch into the bottom of two glasses and handed one to me. "Hair of the dog."

I took it and picked up the picture of Dad from the mantel. It was taken at a church picnic. Smiling, he brandished a barbecue fork. I realized with a start how much I looked like him and also how little this smiling man resembled the one who haunted my nightmares. I sipped the cheap scotch. It burned on the way down, but I was grateful for some liquid courage. I glanced at Al. He was watching me curiously. I put the picture down and walked to the window, which gazed out over the field where the barn used to be.

Gesturing with my glass, I said, "Do you remember that summer you came home from school and you asked me about the TV set up in the barn?"

Al nodded. "You said Dad thought it made the cows produce more. He had some crazy ideas."

I nodded, not looking back at Al. "Yes, he did. But that wasn't one of them."

Al waited. I could feel him behind me, like he'd always been when I was a kid—behind me, protecting me, making sure Dad wasn't too harsh. "It was after you left. I had to have been about twelve." I turned to Al. "Do you remember when Aunt Edith sent Mom a Playgirl magazine as a joke?"

He nodded. "She was so embarrassed she threw it in the garbage straight away."

"Well, I pulled it out." I could still remember brushing coffee grounds from the cover, my hands trembling with a mix of fear and excitement. "I stuffed it under my mattress. Dad found it."

"Oh, man." It came out in a whisper.

"He went crazy. I mean crazy, crazy. Next thing I knew, he'd set up the TV in the barn, and he..." I closed my eyes. When I opened them, Al was beside me. All I saw in my brother's eyes was compassion. I took a deep breath and continued. I was going to get this out if it killed me. "He had these tapes. God knows where he got them. Cheesy gay porn." I shuddered. "Hearing that music still makes me sick. So does that barn smell, cows and shit and hay."

Al stepped forward. He put his arm around me. "He could be a bastard sometimes."

I pressed my eyes shut against the tears. "He used a belt. Said he'd beat the faggot out of me. Made me stand there and watch. And I'd try not to get excited, but…"

"Shhh." Al squeezed my shoulder. "I'm sorry, bro. I should have been here to protect you."

I shook my head. "There was nothing you could do. Nothing anyone could do." I wiped my eyes and laughed. "It worked. Eighties porn is a real turnoff to me."

He patted my arm. "I don't know about the gay stuff, but with straight porn, production quality is better now."

I stared at him. "Don't tell me you watch porn. You're a good churchgoing man."

He shrugged. "Emphasis on man. I've been a widower a long time."

I pulled away from him so that I could meet his eyes. "You understand what I'm telling you, right?"

"That Dad was an abusive man? No news there." Al half smiled. I waited, watching him. "And that you're gay? Sorry, also not news."

I blinked at him, for a moment too shocked to speak.

Al held up his hand. "Granted, we didn't have a clue before we went out to visit you. Mom saw the extra toothbrush in your bathroom. At first we thought it was Cheryl's, but that didn't feel right. Then after the play, the way you looked at Kenny and he looked at you… Well, we all agreed it was his toothbrush."

"Maybe I had two of my own."

Al snorted. "Right, because you're the guy with extra clutter around. So how is Kenny anyway?

"I don't know. I haven't seen him lately. We… I… Well, it didn't work out."

"I'm sorry to hear that. He seemed like a nice guy."

I narrowed my eyes and considered my brother. Maybe I'd stepped into an alternate universe. "Are you telling me you don't have any problem with my being gay?"

He looked away. "I'll admit it's a good thing we didn't talk about it then. It took a while, a lot of talking it out in the family, a lot of prayer, but in the end Jessica convinced us that God doesn't make mistakes. For whatever reason, he made you gay, and we need to be okay with that."

"You've been discussing this in the family?"

He blushed. "Only Mom, Jessica, and me. I'm not sure the cousins and aunties would like it. But it isn't any of their business, is it?"

It felt like mountains of weight had fallen off my shoulders. I was almost giddy with the lightness. "Mom knows."

"She's the one who suggested it." He looked out at the field where the afternoon light was turning the corn a vibrant green. "Now that I know about the barn, it seems like maybe she knew all along, and it wasn't until after Dad died that she could let herself accept it."

"What about New Pentecostal, Brother Howard, and all those people? If I come out more publicly, is it going to affect how things go for you with them?"

He shrugged. "Brother Howard and Dad and some of the others have a harsh view of God." He held up his scotch. "Clearly I don't share them. And neither does Mom."

"Neither does Mom what?" She stood in the doorway wearing a fresh apron, an oven mitt on one hand, the other on her hip.

I turned and said the words I'd practiced a hundred times in Dr. Bernstein's office. "Mom, I'm gay."

She beamed. "Oh, honey, I'm so glad you're telling me."

I almost giggled with relief.

Mom asked, "How's your nice friend Kenny?"

The incipient laughter died. "We're not seeing each other anymore."

Her smile faded. Then she determinedly brightened. "You'll find someone. Don't worry."

"I hope so, Mom." Looking at her, I felt like my heart might burst out of my chest.

As she led the way into the kitchen, where mountains of food were laid out on the kitchen table, she said, "Thank

God California legalized marriage last week. I hate the idea of you living in sin."

I grinned. The more things change, the more things stay the same.

LOS ANGELES

2010: A January Wedding

"I have tickets to a play on Friday night if you want to go." Cheryl was chopping veggies for chili while I made coleslaw. We were catering an afternoon gathering at a producer's house. He'd wanted an all-American picnic to announce his upcoming film. We'd be picking up two dozen apple pies from my pastry chef on the way. The new system worked great. Half the stuff we cooked in the truck, and the rest got completed by a small staff working out of a converted trailer in the middle of an industrial wasteland. Between the low overhead and our portability, we undercut the big catering firms and had more business every day. Which meant my nights off were rare. The last thing I wanted to do on them was mingle with the public.

"Thanks, but I think I'll stay home. How about asking your daughter?"

"New boyfriend. As soon as I said I was willing to spring for a sitter, she was on the phone making plans."

Cheryl shook her head. "Not that I blame her. No one said single motherhood was easy."

"It's not exactly single motherhood if you live with your mom, is it?"

She shrugged. "That might make it easier, but it doesn't make it easy."

We chopped in companionable silence for a while. One of the great things about working with someone for a long time is you don't need all that mindless chatter. One of the bad things is you know, just know, when they have something they're dying to say.

"What?" I asked when I couldn't stand it any longer.

She kept chopping. "I'd really like you to go to the show with me. Get out of the house and all."

I narrowed my eyes and watched her chop. "There's someone you want me to meet. If it's a contact for the business, I'll consider it, but if you're trying to set me up, you know I don't have time for all that."

Cheryl put down her knife, wiped her hands, and reached into the back pocket of her jeans. She pulled out a folded piece of paper and handed it to me.

I brushed my hands on my apron and took it from her. "What's with the drama?"

She gave a little half shrug, half nod.

I unfolded the paper. It was a flyer for Liquid Dreams, a new play by Kenny Marks. I folded it carefully and handed it toward her. "I can't do that, Cheryl. You know I can't."

"They broke up."

I stared. "The doctor?"

Cheryl smiled. "A couple months ago. I had drinks with Kenny last night. He's not exactly broken up about it."

I could barely hear her for the pounding of blood in my ears. I squeezed my eyes closed, willing away the images of Kenny that were cascading through my mind. I opened my eyes to see Cheryl looking at me with concern.

"Are you okay?"

"Yeah. But there's no way he'll want to—"

"You can't know if you don't try." She tapped the folded flyer against the counter. "So what do you say? Are you in or out?"

Was I in or out? Hadn't that always been the question? I took a deep breath and let it out slowly. Time to man up.

"Okay. But if he won't see me, we're getting very drunk afterward. Deal?"

She laughed. "If you're buying, it's a deal."

I nodded, already steeling myself for the rejection I knew was coming.

* * * *

The play was funny enough to occasionally distract me from worrying about whether I should have worn the red sweater instead of the black, which I knew was only my way of keeping my mind from wandering into the dangerous territory of What will Kenny say?

During the intermission I bought Cheryl a glass of wine but decided to save my serious drinking for after the fall. I kept scanning the crowd for Kenny, even though I knew he liked to sit out premiers in the greenroom, away from the judgment of the crowd. If it went well, he'd see the show the second night. If it went badly, he'd avoid the neighborhood for months.

Or at least that had been his theoretical plan. The one show he'd had produced while we were together had been a hit. Later ones had too. Although I'd been too afraid of how much it would hurt to see the plays, or to see him there with someone else, I had a scrapbook full of clippings. On lonely nights I read and reread the reviews more often than I should. I particularly loved the one where the reviewer called him a rising star.

The lights blinked, and ushers herded us back in. I lost myself in the second half, laughing along with the crowd and standing at the end, clapping my hands off. The actors were good, probably the director too. But it was Kenny's vision, Kenny's words that had the audience on their feet. I was so proud of him.

The audience filed toward the doors, and I began to sweat. I turned to Cheryl. "This was a bad idea. We should go."

"Come on. Don't be an idiot." She took my arm and steered me out of the crowd and into the hallway leading backstage.

My heart was pounding, and I could feel the sweat pouring down my spine. I was about to turn and leave when there he was, stepping through a doorway and into the hall. He was laughing with the female lead, his smile even more beautiful than I remembered. He was older, a little rounder, and his hair was different, shorter and streaked with red. Seeing how he'd changed made me ache for the time I'd lost. I stood still, not breathing as I watched him approach.

He looked up, and his smile disappeared when he saw me. Cheryl's grip tightened on my arm, but I barely noticed. All I could do was stare into Kenny's eyes and will him to come over. He said something to the actress. She glanced at us curiously, kissed his cheek, and walked away. Kenny approached slowly.

As he neared, he smiled at Cheryl. "You came. Thanks." He leaned forward and kissed her cheek. He was close enough I could smell his shampoo. I couldn't think of a thing to say. All I wanted to do was reach out and touch him.

He stepped back and turned toward me. "And I see you brought a friend."

"Hi, Kenny," I managed to croak out.

He inclined his head. "You look good. Having your own business suits you."

Cheryl cleared her throat. "I think I left my sweater back in the theater. I'll be right back."

I watched her go. "She wasn't wearing a sweater."

He smiled. "Subtle as a truck, that's our Cheryl."

I felt tongue-tied. There I had him, right in front of me, and except for the need to stay with him, to do anything to keep him from leaving again, my mind was a total blank. He seemed to be waiting for something.

"Cheryl says you broke up with your doctor," I blurted.

Kenny wrinkled his nose. "That sounds like I had a condition or something. I didn't break up with my doctor, but I did leave Jim."

"Sorry, that's how I've been thinking of him since Cheryl first told me you'd found someone. 'Kenny's doctor.'" Fuck. I was babbling. "Can we talk?"

Kenny tipped his head. "We are talking."

"No, I mean somewhere else, somewhere more—"

"Private? I thought we had that conversation a long time ago." He crossed his arms over his chest.

Shit, I'm losing him again.

"No, no, I meant somewhere we can sit, have a glass of wine maybe." I touched his arm, wanting to uncurl that hostility. "Please, Kenny, I've missed you so much. We can go wherever you like, or stay right here. I don't care as long as I get to see you."

I could feel his arm loosening beneath my hand. He bit his lip and considered me.

"Please?" I whispered.

He blew air out. "The cast is getting together at a bar downtown. You can come if you like."

I had to stop myself from kissing him.

He held my gaze. "You sure? They'll assume you're my date."

I ran my hands up his arms and smiled. "Nothing would make me more proud."

He opened his mouth to say something, and then I did kiss him. Lightly, my lips brushing his like a question, like a prayer. And I felt his answering sigh.

The cast party was on the second floor of a downtown bar. I tried to stay close as Kenny sashayed around with a darling-this and a honey-that. My heart pounded. I could feel the flush in my face, but whether it was from excitement over being close to Kenny again, the thought of where the night might end, or residual fear of exposure… I couldn't sort it all out. And frankly, I didn't want to. If my father's fearmongering lingered in my bones, I wanted to ignore it. I'd had years of therapy—an exorcism, really—and now I wanted to react normally, whatever that meant.

Kenny introduced me simply as George. Some nodded hello, others scrutinized me curiously, and at least one young man—a bit player I remembered from the second act—scowled. Kenny didn't pay him any more or less attention than he did anyone else, so I decided his was an unrequited admiration. Just in case the young actor had any doubts as to my feelings, I stood close as breath behind Kenny and let my fingers trail up and down his arm.

Kenny gave me a startled glance, but he didn't move away, and I was hit by a sudden wave of longing for him that almost knocked me off my feet.

The party got wilder as the cast and crew slammed tequila shots. Kenny sipped one glass of wine. I had a club soda. I'd waited a long time for this night. I wasn't going to blow it by drinking too much.

At midnight, Kenny turned to me. "You ready?"

I nodded and entwined my hand in his.

He looked up into my eyes. "This is where I ask, who are you and what have you done with George?"

"I've changed."

"Clearly." He searched my eyes for a moment longer, then disentangled his hand and led me out the door.

The night air was cool. I wished I'd brought a jacket.

Kenny drove the car. But he was wary of me in a way I didn't remember. Or maybe I didn't want to remember those last few weeks together when everything was falling apart.

"Why'd you leave your doctor? I mean, Jim."

He watched me, his expression unreadable. "He was moving to North Carolina and asked me to go with him. It's one thing to stay in a mediocre relationship. It's another to uproot your life so it can continue."

We drove silently for a few more minutes while I tried to think of what to say. "Are you still living with all those roommates?"

"No. They got someone new when I moved in with Jim. I've got a studio in Echo Park." He paused. I waited. "Near you, actually. Or at least where you used to live."

"I'm still there."

He nodded.

The city was always prettiest at night, when the dark hid the trash and dirt and colored lights decorated the streets. I stared into the unshaded windows of a few apartments as we passed. The light from inside the rooms seemed cozy. I imagined couples and families of all sorts living in idyllic happiness. I looked at Kenny, his profile sharp against the passing streetlights.

"I want to start again." It just slipped out. I held my breath and watched him watching the road and chewing his lip.

He tapped his fingers on the steering wheel. "I don't know, George."

I leaned toward him and spoke quickly. "Give me a chance to prove I've changed. Come to dinner with me."

He stiffened. "That's how we got in trouble the first time."

"It'll be different, I promise. I tell you what. Meet me tomorrow night at L'Ouest. I'll book us a table, and we can talk."

His lip twitched into a smile. "At L'Ouest? Aren't we banned from there?"

"Not as customers. If you can't do tomorrow night, any other night. And if you don't like L'Ouest, name any restaurant in the city. Dinner and conversation. That's all I'm asking."

He shook his head. "That's not all you're asking. But okay. Tomorrow night. L'Ouest."

He pulled up in front of my apartment building. I put my hand on his. "I've missed you. I can't even tell you how much."

He stared down at my hand. I almost didn't hear him whisper, "I've missed you too." He looked up, and I held his gaze for a long time.

Eventually he nodded toward the door. "Good night. I'll see you tomorrow."

I opened the door and stepped out, giddy at the thought that he'd agreed to the date.

"You still making doughnuts for the homeless?"

"Every Wednesday morning, rain or shine. A couple of kids from the neighborhood take over when I can't make it."

He held my gaze for a moment, then shooed me away with a wave. As I ran upstairs, I felt as light as air. By the time I got to the balcony he was already gone. But it didn't matter. I was going to see him again. I let out a whoop.

Someone down the street yelled, "Shut up!"

I grinned into the darkness. It didn't matter what anyone thought about anything—Kenny was having dinner with me.

* * * *

Zajac's had an afternoon wedding the next day, a simple affair held in the couple's backyard. Cheryl met me at the warehouse early in the morning as the sun was warming the pavement, and the blue sky seemed to go on forever. Or at least until it hit the buildings on either side of the parking lot.

In answer to Cheryl's raised eyebrows, I said, "I have dinner reservations at eight. If we're late finishing, can you take over?"

She smiled. I mean really smiled. "Where you taking him?"

I think I blushed. "L'Ouest."

"I love it." She laughed. "Stephan is going to shit a brick."

I shrugged. "I don't really care about Stephan. But I hope Kenny is impressed."

* * * *

I left Cheryl cleaning up after the wedding so I'd have time to shower and change. I'd tried on every suit I owned the night before and all of them had seemed dated and were a little baggy. Considering myself carefully in the mirror for the first time in a while, I realized the pudginess was gone. It had slipped away so slowly that I hadn't noticed. Trying on pants with real waistbands rather than elastic romper chef clothes, I could see the difference. I didn't exactly have a six-pack, but I didn't have pouches of fat either. In fact, I looked pretty damned good.

"I'd do ya," I told my reflection. But then who else had I been doing for the past few years?

I called a cab. I didn't want to show up wind ruffled from the bike, and I hoped Kenny might bring me home. Or take me home, for that matter. The city streets thrummed with the same mix of anticipation, excitement, and flat-out terror that I felt. Or maybe that was projection. Either way, the cab seemed to go both too fast and too slow—I thought we'd never get to L'Ouest, and I hoped it would take forever.

Climbing out of the cab, I saw Kenny walking toward me. He was still a block away, having had to stash his car somewhere down the way. A wave of relief washed over me. I'd half expected him to stand me up. I watched him approach, his fluid grace a walking pride poster. I couldn't imagine why I'd been embarrassed to be seen with him. He was handsome and smart, and any man would be lucky to have a chance. It was thoughts like that that emboldened me to greet him with a hug and a light kiss.

He pulled away and cocked one eyebrow. "That's new."

"I'm glad you came." I put my arm around him to lead him into the restaurant.

He glanced at the doorway. "Aren't we supposed to boycott this place? I heard he donated heavily to Prop 8."

"He did. Being Mr. Anti Gay Marriage was the best thing he could have done for my business, and yes, there's a general boycott, but I'm making a point here."

He took a deep breath and nodded. "Okay, it's your show."

It was weird to walk in the front door. All that time I'd spent back in the kitchen, I'd rarely been in the dining room. But I did recognize Curt at the desk.

"Good evening," he started, and then, "Good Lord, look who the cat dragged in."

"Hey, Curt. How are you? Reservation for two—Zajac." I kept my arm around Kenny. I didn't know if it was because it felt as good to him as it did to me or whether he stayed there out of sheer defiance. For the moment I didn't care about his motivation. It felt incredible to touch him.

Curt picked up two menus and gestured toward the back of the restaurant. "Right this way, gentlemen."

I nodded toward the empty table in the front window. It had a reserved sign in the center. "I specifically requested a window table."

Curt paled. "I'm sorry, George, but that's reserved."

Stepping away from Kenny, I peered down at the reservation book. "Yes, it is. Table four reserved for, let me see... That says Zajac, doesn't it?"

Curt's face grew paler. "George, you know this isn't me. I don't care. But Stephan will kill me if I put you guys in the window. He's been even crazier about that sort of thing ever since Prop 8 and the boycott." He glanced at Kenny. "No offense."

Kenny shook his head, but he didn't say anything. He watched me.

I smiled at Curt. "You can tell Stephan that I threatened to sue the restaurant for discrimination if you didn't seat us in the window table, as per our reservation."

Curt opened and closed his mouth. With a shrug, he led us to the window table.

When he had seated us, handed us our menus, and walked out of earshot, Kenny leaned across the table and whispered, "Can you do that? Sue for discrimination based on table placement?"

"I have no idea." I opened my menu. "But I'm betting that Chef Stephan doesn't either."

Kenny chuckled. "You're probably right about that. The menu hasn't changed. How can he get away with that?"

"He gets away with a lot of things he shouldn't. Do you want to order the Steak Diable or crêpes Suzette, something to bring him out of the kitchen to flambé at our table?"

Kenny smiled but shook his head. "Let's not spoil the evening with a visit from Stephan. I've always wanted to try the ham-and-fig tartines. You want to split an order?"

Restaurants have high staff turnover, especially among the waitstaff. Other than Curt, there didn't appear to be anyone working whom we'd known before. Which was just as well. I'd had a reunion in mind for the evening, but not that kind. We ended up ordering three appetizers and two entrées. When I added an expensive bottle of wine, I had to assure Kenny that business was good, and I could afford a night out.

"Besides," I added, "I haven't exactly been Mr. Romeo the past few years. I've earned a splurge."

He sat back in his chair and considered me. "Cheryl told me you haven't dated anyone since we broke up."

I smiled. "I wondered whether the two of you talked about me."

Kenny laughed. "Sort of like passing notes in junior high, isn't it?"

The wine steward arrived to pour with the usual ceremony. When he left, I lifted my glass. "To an amazing playwright. Congratulations on another success."

"Thank you." He clinked my glass. "You're not doing badly for yourself either."

I looked around the restaurant. "For that I can thank Stephan. If he hadn't fired us, I think I might have stayed on for years." I caught Kenny's gaze and held it. "Especially if I could be close to you."

Kenny sipped wine and watched me over his glass. "As friends with benefits?"

I grimaced. "I was an idiot."

"I'll grant you that."

Food came, which gave us an excuse to drop that subject.

Kenny bit into a tartine and licked his fingers. The sight of his finger slipping into his mouth sent a bolt of excitement straight to my cock. It was a good thing we were sitting down. Whatever was on my face made him smile and slowly lick another.

I sighed.

He wiped his fingers on his napkin and leaned forward. "You're an alien from a gay-friendly planet, and you've taken over my old friend George's body, right?"

I laughed. "I wish it was that easy. Would have saved me a bundle in therapy bills."

He rested his elbows on the table. "Tell me."

And so I did. Through the appetizers and into the main course I told him about my father, the barn, my marriage, and the fear that had rung like a baseline through my life. He didn't ask questions, but nodded and gestured for me to continue whenever I slowed down. I watched his face for signs of disgust as I let him know my weakness. But his eyes held only compassion.

When I finished, he looked away, out at the street. A man and a woman stood reading the menu by the restaurant door. She seemed unhappy, or maybe tired and hungry. It can be so difficult to read another person's mind.

Kenny caught my eye again. "I was hard on you back then."

"No." It came out so loudly that a couple at the next table glanced over. I lowered my voice. "You were very patient. I treated you badly. I promise, it won't happen again."

Kenny played with a piece of bread, pulling off bits and dropping them onto his plate. Frown lines sliced his forehead. "I don't know, George. Do you think it's possible for people to hit Reset?"

I reached across the table and touched his hands. He stopped shredding bread and considered me. "We can try. You were right. I was in love with you. I still am."

There was a sound to our left. Kenny glanced over. His face hardened. I followed his gaze. Chef Stephan was making his rounds.

Kenny started to pull away. I gripped his hands more firmly. "Fuck him," I whispered. "I'm done kowtowing to homophobic bullies."

Kenny nodded. He raised our hands to his lips and kissed my fingers.

Chef Stephan stepped close to our table and hissed, "Stop that. It's disgusting. What are you doing in my restaurant?"

Kenny smiled into my eyes. "Don't worry. We won't be back. George here called for a do-over, and this was where we had to start."

I looked up at Stephan, whose face was blooming in a way that let me know that if we'd been back in the kitchen, he would have been yelling, tossing cookware, and making grown men cower. But out here in the glare of public opinion, he pressed his lips together and walked stiffly away.

"Do you want to stay for dessert?" I asked Kenny, who still held my hand.

He shook his head. "I bet we can find something better back at my place."

I signaled to the waiter that we were ready for the bill.

* * * *

Kenny pulled up to an adobe house on a quiet side street. He led me around the back and down a short flight of stairs. I stood behind him as he opened the door, breathing in the scent of him mixed with the dusty scent of old concrete.

He smiled over his shoulder. "Welcome to my humble abode."

It was a small studio, crowded but clean, with grill-covered windows set high along one wall. The only clutter involved piles of paper stacked next to a computer on an otherwise tidy desk. The kitchen was defined by a strip of linoleum on the floor beside a tiled counter with a microwave, a sink, and a built-in dorm-sized refrigerator.

He looked around, as if appraising it for the first time. "It's not much, but I only have to work part-time to support myself here, which gives me more time to write."

I glanced at the Asian-style screen that hid the sleeping area. "I like it. It's cozy."

Kenny laughed. "Don't give me that. You hate it. It's cluttered. But look what I have that you don't have." He gestured to the corner of the room. "A couch." He looked uncertain. "Or maybe you do have a couch by now."

I shook my head. "No couch."

"You want anything?" Kenny moved into the kitchen area.

"Uh-huh, I do." I slipped off my jacket and hung it over a chair, along with my tie. I walked over to the couch and sat down. "But you're not going to find it in the kitchen."

"Oh, I'm not? Where will I find it?" He came toward me, and my breath caught. He let his own jacket drop with a slow, sexy shrug. He stood there in a long-sleeved black T-shirt and dark jeans, looking hip and smooth. When he got close enough I grabbed his hand and pulled him down on the couch beside me.

"You've changed your shampoo," I whispered, inhaling the smell of his hair.

"Probably." He ran his fingers over my belly. "You've changed more than your attitudes. Look at you. You're ripped."

I caught his mouth with mine. Lips first, tasting him behind the wine and food, the Kenny-ness. He shifted against me, leaning into the kiss. I let my tongue push into his mouth, and he opened to me with the softest moan. I ran my fingers through his hair and held the back of his head, pulling him to me with a hunger that surprised even me.

Kenny's hands moved from my belly to my chest. His fingers brushed my nipples through the thin fabric of my good shirt.

Our breath sounded loud in the small apartment. Kenny felt warm in my arms. I wanted to kiss him forever, slow and sweet and remembering. Except that the more he touched me, the tighter my pants got, and the more that particular region of my body cried out for attention.

Kenny pulled away, but not very far away. He searched my face. "You even kiss differently. Who have you been with since me?"

"No one in a long time. At first I hit the bars, but it only made me miss you more afterward." I dug in my pocket and brought out the piece of paper I'd been carrying all night like a hopeful teenager with a pack of condoms. I handed it to him. "This time I know what to bring to a first date with you."

He unfolded my test results and skimmed them with a smile. He leaned down to the floor, picked up his jacket, and rummaged in the inside pocket. "I've got one for you too. I almost didn't. I thought maybe that would keep me from bringing you home. Help my resolve."

I dropped the paper on the floor and cupped his face. "I'm glad you changed your mind. If you're going to feel bad about this, I can still go."

"Are you kidding?" He grabbed my hand and pressed it to his crotch. He felt rock hard.

I groaned, and whatever gentlemanly restraint I'd been exhibiting came apart. I dived for his lap, my fingers fumbling at the zipper of his pants while he stroked my back. He shifted, and I slid his pants to his knees. He was wearing dark blue briefs. I paused to relish the sight of dark hair on his pale thighs and to appreciate the moment.

I took in the smell of soap and flesh. "It's like an unveiling," I whispered, grasping the waistband of his underwear.

Kenny looked down with a laugh. "Except it's nothing you haven't seen before."

"Hmm. But it is something I intend to worship." His cock popped out as I pulled down his briefs.

I wrapped my hand around it. "Hello," I whispered. "How've you been?"

"Lonely," Kenny said in a high-pitched voice.

I looked at him. "Your dick is a soprano?"

He shrugged. "You got a problem with that?"

"No way." I licked the tip, savoring the taste.

Kenny sighed. His fingers brushed my hair. "Do you need me to—"

I shook my head. "Let me try this on my own." I held the base tight as I slid my lips down his shaft. Pulling back up with suction felt like a sensory feast.

I couldn't believe how good he tasted, like a spring day at the beach, and how good it felt to take him all the way in, then to slide slowly back up the shaft. He smelled so familiar, like coming home, only it was different, tender, heartbreaking even, and I couldn't imagine why I'd wanted it any other way. Kenny stroked my hair so gently I thought I might cry.

"Wait. Sit up for a sec," he whispered. "I want to taste you too."

I came off him reluctantly, lingering for one last second to tongue the inverted V of his cockhead. The sound he made—half sigh, half moan—sent a bolt of excitement straight through me.

I sat up and kissed him, thrusting my tongue deep into his mouth. He answered by caressing my tongue with his, and then we were trading back and forth, like a dance.

He pushed me away. "Jesus. Oh, shit, George. Take your clothes off now. I want to feel you."

I stripped so fast I heard a button pop. I was too riveted by the sight of Kenny peeling out of his shirt to care about anything but feeling him and tasting him.

He'd barely kicked out of his jeans when I attacked him again, letting my whole body participate in the kiss. His skin against mine felt like a miracle. I wanted to press inside him, to crawl into Kenny like I was going home.

When I took him in my mouth, Kenny slid down my body, nudging me until we both lay cock to mouth, cradled between each other's legs.

Of course I'd felt Kenny's mouth on me before but always with me tied or commanded in the rough, forced way I'd demanded of him. This equal give-and-take of spit and cock was both exciting and terrifyingly intimate. I concentrated on the smell of his skin and on the taste of his cock, the feel of it filling my mouth, the ridges of his veins beneath my tongue until the fear subsided and I could allow myself to feel his lush, wet mouth around me. I matched my rhythm to his, and everything else disappeared, in a way it never had before, so that there was only Kenny and me, his cock, my mouth, my cock, his mouth, the smell of skin, the wet sounds of our lips and tongues, the friction of worn cloth where my hip and shoulder rubbed the couch. Kenny breathed in little huffs. The sound of blood pounding in my ears seemed to fill the room.

It was familiar and different. It suddenly seemed symbolic that I was turned around and had him in my mouth from an altogether new direction. And yet he smelled the same and felt the same, and I watched as his balls tightened as they always had before he came. He moaned, the sound reverberating around my cock, and I was falling into him, sucking every drop as he filled my mouth with sweet, salty Kenny, my own orgasm a surprise I hadn't been thinking about, but there it was, following Kenny's like a shadow, and I was pulsing into him, gripping his thighs with spasming fingers as I swallowed everything he spilled into my mouth.

When it was over, we continued to lie like that, each with his head on the other's inner thigh, our other legs propped like bookends.

Kenny's eyes were soft. "Hi."

"Hey."

We watched each other breathe for a while.

Kenny smiled sadly. "A little bit of this would have made a difference."

"I know. I'm sorry. Can't promise I'll always be perfect. I've been messed up for a long time. But I want to make you happy."

He stroked the inside of my thigh. "Tonight you've done that." A surge of hope ran through me. Kenny frowned.

"I was unhappy with you for a long time, though. I'm not promising anything."

I ran my hand over his beautiful flank. "Fair enough. Do you want me to stay or go?"

He chewed his lower lip and watched my eyes. "Stay."

That was a relief. Feeling the need to lighten things up, I closed my legs over his head and squeezed lightly. "Aha, I have you now."

"Let go." His voice was muffled. "Don't suffocate me with your sweaty balls."

I raised my thigh and looked at him. "But you love sweaty balls."

"You got me there. I do love sweaty balls." He leaned forward and licked mine.

This was what happiness felt like. I closed my eyes to seal the moment in my memory. The past was gone and the future unknown, and the present was a gift.

Thank you for the insight, Dr. Bernstein.

2010: A March Wedding

In Los Angeles, like anywhere else, it was all about who you knew. I knew Libby, which kept me in weddings, and I knew Kenny, who knew the theater community. With my mobile kitchen I was light on my feet and could travel. One morning, out for coffee at Kenny's favorite haunt, we ran into a producer whose wedding I'd catered a few years earlier and whose doors Kenny had knocked on more recently. The planets slid into alignment, and I got the opportunity to bid on my first movie, catering a production scheduled to start the next year.

I shook my head in wonder. "A solid month of work. I wonder if Cheryl will go for it."

"A month away from me." Kenny made an exaggerated pouty face. "You should wonder whether I'll go for it."

"You could come with me. All that time in a nice air-conditioned hotel room in Arizona with me away all day. Think how much work you'd get done."

He raised his eyebrows. "Hmm. Of course I'd have to quit my job."

"Maybe by then you'll have hit it big. If not, you can take a vacation. Find fill-ins. It's not like some of the other waiters don't owe you favors. I know they do. I worked with you, remember?"

He stretched and gestured for another foamy coffee drink. "We'd need to be back by Purim."

I laughed. "You're scheduling parties a year in advance now?"

"How different is that from you scheduling my vacation next year?" He stared down at his empty cup. "You're coming, right? To Purim? This year?"

"Are you kidding? You think I'd miss it? That worked out so well for me last time."

He looked up at me and smiled. "Good. Have you thought about your costume? Technically you can come as anything, but I always feel like since I'm on the planning committee I should come as something traditional."

"Whatever you say."

"Good. Your choices are Haman—he's the bad guy, and that's a cool costume because if you're Haman, every time someone says your name people hiss—Ahasuerus, the king Esther seduces; Mordecai, her uncle and pimp; and my favorite, Queen Esther herself."

"This is a religious holiday?"

He nodded. "Even the super religious celebrate it. Great holiday. The best part is you're commanded to get drunk."

"Combining sex, religion, and alcohol wouldn't have gone over well in my family of origin."

Kenny waved his hand at me. "Nothing fun would have gone over well with them. It's all kosher, based on a Bible story. Or maybe it's a story that didn't make it into the Bible. I forget. Look it up—the Book of Esther. Sex, lies, and intrigue."

I shook my head. "I guess every religion has its weird traditions. I'll go as whoever you think I should."

He cocked his head to one side and considered me. "You'd make a handsome Ahasuerus. On the other hand, I'm not sure I want all those pretty Queen Esthers throwing themselves at you. You're too blond for Haman and Mordecai. Well, you don't look Jewish enough." A wicked grin spread across his face. "You'd make a lovely queen."

I sputtered out the sip of coffee I'd been taking. Mopping it up, I frowned at him. "I fell right into that, didn't I?"

"You did say you'd go as anything I wanted." His smile was playful, but it still felt like a test. How far would I go for him? Would I have coffee every possible morning in his favorite, very public spot? Would I go out dancing, dining, walking in the park? Could we have our pictures taken together? And now, would I go to his party dressed as a queen?

I liked tests, as long as I knew how to pass them. I had a lot to prove to both of us. "Fine. But no heels. I work on my feet and can't afford a broken ankle."

"Fair enough, although you might surprise yourself. And heels would do great things for your calves." He threw down the last of his fresh cup of coffee and pushed back from the table. "Let's go shopping."

"Right now?"

"Why not? We only have two weeks, and you don't get that many days off."

Shit. What have I done? I followed him out of the coffee shop.

* * * *

The thrift store—a giant box of a room filled with long racks of clothes—smelled of dust and air freshener. Shelves full of dishes and small appliances spanned one wall. Banks of shoes filled a corner.

Kenny led me directly to a tall rack filled with long dresses—satin and chiffon. Two middle-aged women who were thumbing through children's clothes looked over at us. One said something to the other, who shook her head. I fought a wave of embarrassment and terror. I was a man in my forties, not a terrified little boy. They were strangers I'd never see again, not members of my father's church. What they thought didn't matter. I needed to focus on something that did.

Kenny was riffling through the dresses and talking nonstop. "I'd lend you something of mine—I've been Esther lots in the past—but they'd all be too short. And you're so broad-shouldered. I think size 16 at least. Aren't women's sizes strange? They have nothing to do with measurements. What does sixteen mean? It's not like size 32 pants. You know what the thirty-two in that means. Here, what do you think of this?"

He held up a pastel-pink creation in satin and chiffon, layers and layers of chiffon.

I laughed and pointed to the enormous cups. "I couldn't fill those."

He brushed my comment away with his hand. "That's what socks are for. Here, hold it, and we'll see what else there is in your size."

And so I stood in an aisle of a brightly lit thrift store in downtown Los Angeles while Kenny filled my arms with frothy dresses. Hardly anyone paid attention to us. Of the few who did, as many smiled as scowled, and I realized that the world wouldn't end if my secret got out. In fact, I didn't want to have a secret. I wanted the whole world to know I was in love.

Kenny draped another dress over my arms, and I leaned forward and kissed him, right there in front of God and everyone.

When he pulled away, Kenny had a funny half smile. "What was that all about?"

"Dunno. Maybe I'm getting into my part. If I'm Queen Esther, who will you be?"

He wiggled his eyebrows at me. "Haman. I figure if you're stepping out of your comfort zone, I can too. I'll swagger around all night like a pirate. And everyone will hate me."

"Except me. I won't hate you."

"But you're Queen Esther. You're supposed to hate me."

"Not this Queen Esther. I think she has a thing for pirates. I suppose you want me to try these on."

He nodded happily. "Let's hang these near the dressing rooms and go look for pirate gear. Or maybe biker. Which do you think looks badder? Hey, do you think these pants would make my ass look hot?"

"I've never seen you in anything that didn't."

"Flatterer." He practically skipped toward the dressing room.

I paused, shocked to realize that I was having fun. I looked down at the load of colorful, slippery, gauzy stuff I had piled in my arms. Who knew?

* * * *

I'd declined a small catering job in order to be free all day before the Purim party. As I pulled up at Kenny's apartment building, I remembered another Purim party day. It seemed crazy that I would have sacrificed so much for so little.

"I brought bagels. You know, because they're Jewish." I thrust the bag toward him to cover my lame joke. I hadn't realized how nervous I was until he opened the door. It was one thing to try on dresses in a seedy downtown store where no one I knew was around, and another to go to a party wearing pink chiffon.

He opened the bag and inhaled. "Nice. They smell like the real thing." Then he leaned close to me and inhaled again. "So do you. I love that windy, gas-fume smell you get when you've been on the bike."

"But you hate my motorcycle."

"I know." He sniffed my neck. The warmth of his breath sent a shiver down my spine. "It's dangerous and loud and the helmet does terrible things to your hair, but it does make you smell sexy. Very manly."

I laughed, wrapping my arms around him to pull him close. "You're trying to make up for the fact you're about to dress me up like a giant doll."

"Hmmm. Maybe. Is it working?" He slipped his hand down to feel my crotch. "Yes, I think it is."

His mouth met mine, and I slid my hands down to cup his ass. He pushed into me, and I fell against the door, bringing him with me. The wood was cool against my back, as cool as Kenny was hot against my chest. He ground his pelvis into mine. The sound of our jeans brushing together, the feel of his cock hard against mine, and the insistence of his tongue in my mouth rocketed through me.

We broke for air, both of us already breathing hard.

"That's quite a greeting." I loved the way Kenny's skin flushed when he got excited.

He waved the bagel bag, his other hand fumbling with my belt. "Breakfast can wait, don't you think?"

"Oh, yes."

We pulled away and started unbuttoning, unzipping, and dropping clothes as we both moved to the bed behind the screen. Kenny jumped onto the bed first, and I watched him as I finished undressing. I loved the contrast of his dark body hair against pale skin. For the part of the evil Haman, he'd dyed his hair black with one of those temporary dyes. As I took in the effect, I realized it was probably as close to his natural hair color as I was likely to see. It didn't matter what he did with his hair. He was still the most striking man I'd ever known. I let my gaze travel down to his cock, a hard, beautiful tree rising from a dark thicket.

"Hey, slowpoke. You coming to bed or not?"

I kicked out of my shoes, dropped my pants, and threw myself at him. God, the miracle of his skin—smooth in spots, rough with hair on his chest and thighs. Kenny rolled beneath me. His hands felt warm and exciting as he stroked my back. I rubbed my cock against his—swordplay for my pirate. His hands settled on my ass, pulling me against him in a slow rhythm. We could have kept going like that, building to a sweet crescendo, but this was my day to step out of my careful boundaries, so I broke away and slid off him.

Kenny rolled on his side and rested his hand on my hip. He looked at me with concern, which wasn't unreasonable. He had plenty of experience of me as a sexual nut job. "You okay?"

I nodded while I tried to get the words out over the fear and embarrassment that seemed to appear out of nowhere. I could feel my erection wilting as I stuttered and blushed. Taking a deep breath, I willed myself to calm down and talk.

I looked directly into Kenny's kind, worried eyes. "I want you to fuck me."

He blinked. That was good. At least this time around I wasn't boring him.

"Are you sure? I mean, of course I'd love that, you know I would, but it's okay if—"

"No, I want it." I rested my hand on his chest. "It scares the hell out of me, but it's…it's a gift you've been giving me for a long time. I need to reciprocate."

He held my gaze. I tried to relax and let him read my face, see everything I was feeling—the fear, the love, and the need to move on from the past.

"Have you ever done this before?"

I laughed. "Are you kidding? Trust me, there's nothing I've done with anyone else that I haven't done with you. You know exactly how sexually adventurous I'm not."

Kenny cupped the side of my face. "This is a sweet thing you're trusting me with. Thank you."

I turned my head and kissed his palm. "You're my pirate, right?"

Kenny laughed. "Yes, my queen."

He reached across me to get the lube from where it sat on the bedside table on my side of the bed. He kissed me, a long, slow, sweet kiss.

"Roll over on your side," he whispered. "It'll be easier. And pull your knees up."

I did as he said. He started kissing my neck, my shoulders, and my back. He wrapped an arm around me, his hand resting in the center of my chest. With one finger of his other hand he circled the pucker of my ass.

"I love you." It was the first time he'd said it since that morning in his kitchen years ago. I turned my head to look at him, but he stopped me. "Shhh. Relax."

I concentrated on breathing and told myself that no matter what happened, no one had ever died from getting fucked. Or at least not by someone who loved them. Loved them. Kenny still loved me. My heart under his hand seemed to expand, bursting from my chest and filling the room.

Kenny's finger slid into me, and I gasped at how good it felt. My focus narrowed to the slip and slide of his finger in me, hot and dirty. A second finger and goddamn, it still felt good. I gripped the pillow under my head and pushed back into him. Kenny's breath quickened in my ear. His hand moved from my chest to my cock, and I was rocking back and forth, between his fingers in my ass and his hand on my cock.

"Please." God, was that me? I sounded so needy. And that made me even hotter. "Please, Kenny, fuck me, please."

"Oh, yeah." Kenny's voice was husky.

His fingers slipped out of me. Fear washed over me again as I felt the tip of his cock against my ass.

He pushed in. Pain. I tried to move away, but he held me in place.

"It's okay, honey. Don't be afraid."

I bit my lip. If this was what the tip felt like, I was going to die when he shoved the whole thing in. Kenny stayed where he was and brushed my neck and shoulder with light kisses. No, I wasn't going to die. I took a deep breath, let it out, and did it again. On the third breath my muscles relaxed, and pain morphed into desire.

"More," I whispered. Kenny's hand began moving on my cock again. I pushed back, and he slid in another inch, then another, until eventually I could feel his balls against the backs of my thighs.

"You have no idea how good you feel right now," he whispered. "Let me know when you want me to move."

I clenched and unclenched my ass muscles, making him gasp. "Yes. Please."

With a groan, Kenny began to move, slowly at first, then faster, stroking me in rhythm with the pound of his cock in my ass.

I arched into him, completely captivated by the pleasure-pain duet. My world shrank to Kenny's cock, his hand, the slap of his balls against my ass, and the soft flutter of his lips on my neck, my shoulder. I was only vaguely aware that I was talking, begging, words pouring out of me in a steady, slutty, needy torrent. The tangy smell of cow shit disappeared as if Kenny were pounding it away, each stroke erasing the sting of my father's belt. And then I was flying high above the barn, above the bed, leaping out of my body for a single frightened moment before slamming back inside, back to the moment and Kenny's hand, his cock, the blood hammering through me, our breath coming in twin gasps, my balls tightening as I felt the pulse of blood in his cock change, and I was clawing at the bedclothes and shouting and splashing all my love out onto the sheets as Kenny poured his into me.

We lay glued together, our breath and hearts slowing.

Kenny shifted. "As the nurse said before she gave him a shot, you're going to feel a little"—he pulled away, and I winced—"sting."

I rolled onto my back so I could look at him.

He stayed on his side, his head propped in one hand. "How are you?"

I smiled up at him. "Didn't you tell me Queen Esther was supposed to be a virgin at the beginning of the night?"

He ran a finger along my jaw. "Virginity's overrated, don't you think? Shall we take a shower and have some breakfast?"

"Nap first?" I curled into him. Before he could answer, I fell asleep.

* * * *

"Okay, beautiful, time to put on your face." Kenny pushed me into his desk chair and draped a towel over the front of my dress.

"There's something digging into my back. How do women wear these things?"

Kenny stuck his hand down the back of the dress, and the gouging sensation stopped, replaced by vague discomfort at how tightly the material fit around my chest.

"It's the cost of beauty. Now quit squirming." He smoothed the fabric across my lap before straddling it. He examined my face, turning my head one way and then the other. "You have great skin."

"Thank you. Does that mean I can go as I am?"

He scowled at me. "Don't be ridiculous. This is a beauty pageant, after all. You want to look your best. The competition includes some very experienced queens."

My heart started pounding. "What do you mean, competition? I thought this was a costume party."

He brushed something from beneath my eye. "Oh, did I forget to mention the pageant? Silly me. I'm so forgetful sometimes."

"Oh, Christ. What have you suckered me into?" I was not going to panic. As discreetly as possible, I started one of Dr. Bernstein's breathing techniques.

Kenny's tone was teasing. "Just a little stage show. Maybe some lip-synching and an impromptu bit of theater. It'll be fun."

I started to protest, then thought better of it and gritted my teeth. My fears had already cost me too much. In for a penny, in for a pound.

Kenny handed me a wineglass and reached for an open bottle I hadn't noticed on his desk. "I picked this up the other day. A nice Californian zinfandel. I think you'll like it."

I sniffed. Meaty with cherry overtones. I took a long sip. Truth was, at that moment I would have drunk anything. It wasn't shaping up to a good day to be sober. "Nice. Thank you."

Kenny smiled at me. "You are being such a good boy. I'm proud of you. Now tip up your face, and I'll apply foundation."

Foundation sounded like cement. But Kenny's hands felt warm and gentle as they slathered whatever it was on my face. I closed my eyes and enjoyed the feel.

Something cool touched my eyelid, and I blinked open. Kenny held a compact in one hand and a tiny brush in the other. "Should have told you to keep your eyes closed. Now you've smeared it."

"Sorry." I closed my eyes. He swabbed my eyelid with something wet, presumably cleaning up, and started again.

I was startled by a memory. "I'd forgotten, but I used to like to play in my mom's stuff when I was little. She had this lipstick that smelled like perfume."

"I think I know what you mean. Sort of a soapy floral scent. My aunt's kisses always smelled like that."

"I loved it. Whenever they went somewhere and left Al to babysit, I'd sneak into my mom's room and play with her lipstick, sniff it, roll it in and out of the tube, that sort of thing. Al was always too busy watching sports or hanging out with a girlfriend to pay any attention. But then one night my dad came home early."

Kenny stopped brushing my eyelids. I opened my eyes to see him watching me with compassion.

"It wasn't like I'd put it on. I was always too afraid I'd get caught to use the damned stuff. But seeing me with her makeup made him crazy." I took another sip of Kenny's good red wine. "That was the first time he took me out to the barn. It was before he had the TV and the whole complicated setup out there. He beat the crap out of me."

Kenny rested his hand on my chest. "You poor thing."

"I was just a kid playing around." I blinked at the tears pooling around my lashes. "Oh, shit. I'm sorry. I think I messed up your masterpiece."

He shook his head. "I can fix it."

I closed my eyes. He was right. Kenny could fix anything. Even me.

"I was a real makeup hound as a kid." He slid a finger or maybe a thumb over one lid. "Drove my parents crazy, but bless their souls, they didn't make it into a big deal. I think they hoped I'd grow out of it." He shifted on my lap. "Keep your eyes closed. I'm about to glue on your lashes, and you have to stay very still. That's good. So anyway, after I came out and my mom got all involved in Pflag, she came home one night and sat me down. 'Kenny,' she said, all serious, 'there was a boy at the meeting tonight with the most atrocious makeup. You must promise me you'll always be tasteful and never, ever wear blue eye shadow.'"

I cracked up.

He swatted me. "Stop laughing. You'll mess up the line. All right. Open up. It's time for your mascara."

I opened my eyes and looked into his. How was it physically possible to love someone this much?

"Kenny, will you marry me?"

He stopped, mascara wand held high. "I'm sure you don't mean that, but if you did, I'd remind you that it's illegal in this state again, and I'd tell you it's still too early for me to be sure of you yet."

"I am serious. It's legal in Iowa, and we could have the wedding in my mother's backyard. Whenever you're ready."

He held my gaze for a long time. "I'll take it under consideration. In the meantime, I'd be willing to think about pooling our resources so we could get a place together. Somewhere with a real bedroom."

I squeezed his thighs. "How about with two bedrooms, one for your office with a door that locks?"

He smiled. "What a good memory you have. If you promise not to crash in there and read my half-baked ideas, it doesn't need to lock. A door that closes would be lovely, though."

"Let's start looking right away."

Kenny smoothed the shoulder of my gown. "Maybe we should wait until tomorrow, when we're more suitably dressed." He leaned down to kiss me, which messed up my makeup, but neither of us seemed to care.

* * * *

I paused climbing out of Kenny's car and onto the sidewalk in my pink gown and poufy blonde wig. I pictured the expressions on my father's, my mother's, my brother's, and even sweet little Jessica's faces if they could see me parading through town in drag. I should have felt mortified, but instead, I started to giggle. Kenny appeared, looking dashing in black tights, a red-and-gold tunic, and a giant pirate hat, complete with plume. He put one foot in front of the other, doffed his hat, and bowed low.

"Madam?" He held out his hand.

I took it and probably leaned harder on his arm than a lady should, but it was difficult getting out of that tiny car in a huge dress. The shiny silver "ballet flats" Kenny had insisted on when I vetoed heels turned out to be almost as hard to walk in. The soles slid across any surface, which made me think ballet was a euphemism for the kind of tripping around I'd be doing all evening.

A group of bystanders stopped to gawk. I pulled myself up to my full height, thrust out my ridiculously inflated chest—what had Kenny been going for, a Dolly Parton look-alike?—and placed my hand on top of Kenny's. I was a queen, and fuck 'em if they couldn't take a joke.

Since Kenny was on the organizational committee, we'd come to the bar early to help set up. The place was pretty empty, a few regulars and a handful of men in costume. A scattering of applause greeted us as we entered. I pitched my chin toward the ceiling, let Kenny walk me to the center of the room, where he let go of my hand, and I twirled in a slow, majestic circle to hoots, whistles, and catcalls.

The bartender called out, "Hey, Queen Esther, the first one's on the house. What'll it be?"

I batted my false eyelashes at him. "A Pink Lady, of course."

More hoots and laughter, and I realized I was having a fabulous time.

Compared with a standard catering job, there wasn't much setup involved. Which was good since I was hardly dressed for work. I sipped my Pink Lady and watched my Haman throw a few streamers around and set up a long table across the back wall for food. Hors d'oeuvres for the party were potluck, with Zajac's contributing several platters of our signature spicy drumsticks and crudité. Kenny and I had delivered them earlier, before getting dressed up. Once I brought them out from the back, my job was done.

A makeshift stage was set up in one corner of the bar. I stared at it and ordered another Pink Lady. I laid my credit card on the bar. "It's going to be a long night. I better start a tab."

Kenny slid onto the stool next to mine. "Having fun?"

"Hmm." I looked at the bartender and nodded toward Kenny. "That's for whatever this adorable and cunning pirate is having too."

Kenny laughed. "I'm driving. Better give me a soda."

I shook my head. "No, you're not. If I'm going to make an ass out of myself, you're getting drunk with me. Give the nice man your keys. We're taking a cab home."

Kenny passed his keys to the bartender with a shrug. "You're supposed to get so drunk you can't tell the difference between Mordecai and Haman. Make sure you go home with the right guy."

I toasted him with my Pink Lady, sloshing only a little onto my gloves. "I might not know whether you're Haman or Mordecai, but I know who I'm going home with."

By the time the place got crowded, I was far from sober. Cheryl showed up in a slutty little number, black stockings, short skirt, and all, wearing a sign around her neck announcing she was "another rejected virgin."

I laughed when I saw her. "You're as convincing a virgin as I am a queen."

"George?" She peered at me. "I didn't recognize you. You look great, actually."

"I feel ridiculous, but I'm having a ball. Don't tell Kenny. I mean, Haman. I don't want him to know he was right."

She put her hand on my arm and pointed to a little booth set up on one wall. "You should get your picture taken. Really, I can't believe how good you look."

Kenny appeared and gave her a half hug. "I missed my calling as a makeup artist, don't you think? But she's right. Let's commemorate the night I created a monster." He leaned closer to Cheryl. "He's having way too much fun. I may never get him out of women's clothes."

"I bet you can get him out of any clothes, darling." She grinned at him and drifted away.

The photo booth turned out to have a painted background vaguely reminiscent of the drawings of Israel in my Sunday school classrooms. I stood next to Kenny. Right before the photographer pressed the button, I whispered, "My ass still stings."

I stared at the picture once it was printed. Kenny looked gorgeous and dashing, and his smile was a little dangerous. Beside him I looked oddly attractive, in an overblown, big-boned-blonde kind of way.

He took the picture from me. "We'll put this with the keys, shall we? And I need another drink."

Around midnight someone rang a bell, and the music quieted. A tall, thin man in full tux and tails took the stage. He held a microphone and tapped it until the conversations stopped.

"Okay, ladies, gentlemen, and everyone else. It is time to pick our Queen Esther." He held up a sheet of paper. "To qualify, each entrant was required to fill out an extensive questionnaire. We'll be sharing their answers to important, and very personal, questions throughout the evening."

I looked at Kenny. He beamed at me. Very personal? I started to sweat. Fear flooded me. I couldn't breath. I needed to leave. A group of gorgeous drag queens lined up by the stage. Beautiful men with elegant movements. I couldn't breathe.

"George, George," Kenny was whispering in my ear. I looked around for the exit. Kenny's grip on my arm tightened, and I focused on him. "George, I didn't enter you in this. I swear I didn't."

I blinked at him, trying to take in what he was saying. "But you said—"

"I was jerking your chain. Look at those girls." He gestured toward the string of beauties waiting their turn to take the stage. "This isn't Des Moines. This is Los Angeles. Do you really think I'd make you get up onstage with the likes of that? I'm not an asshole."

Relief washed through me. Of course Kenny wouldn't humiliate me. He'd always been my best protector. I pulled him close and put all my relief, my gratitude, and my love into the kiss.

From the stage I heard the pounding of the microphone again. "Turn the lights over there." I kept kissing Kenny even as my shoulder heated up and the light turned the insides of my eyelids pink. "We have a Queen Esther kissing Haman." At the sound of his name the room erupted in hisses and feet pounding on the floor. "Stop that immediately. Don't you know he's the bad guy? You're betrothed to the king."

I pulled away and looked directly into the spotlight. "Are you telling me I can't marry the person I love? Fuck you."

The room exploded into cheers and whoops and barks of approval. I smiled down at Kenny and leaned back into our kiss.

IOWA

2013: A May Wedding

It took him three years to say yes.

* * * *

I stood in front of the mirror in my childhood bedroom thinking that this tux had looked much better in the Des Moines rental shop. But that may have been because when we picked them, I'd been looking at how well it suited Kenny. I felt like an impostor in the sleek black collarless coat and the pink vest, tie, and matching pocket silk. "Maybe I should have gotten something simpler."

My no-longer-only-gay-friend David considered me. He looked pretty cool himself in a gray suit that showed off his spectacular tan. "Stop messing with your tie. You look great."

"I didn't think I'd be this nervous. Of course, last time I got married I was sick for a week ahead of time."

"That should have been a sign for you. Here, I think the boutonniere goes on the left." He pinned it on me and stood back to look.

I stared at him. "I don't think I've ever seen you this happy."

His face brightened. "Ain't love grand?"

"It's not going to bother John to do the ceremony, is it? I mean, bring back bad memories or anything?"

David shrugged. "John's all in favor of marriage. He's happy to do it."

I turned back to the mirror and fiddled with my jacket. "Last time I wore a white tux."

"How virginal."

I laughed. "I looked ridiculous then too. I think. My memory is pretty vague. I got thoroughly drunk."

"But this time you're marrying the man of your dreams." David put his hand on my shoulder. "You ready?"

I took one last look in the mirror. Kenny knew what he was getting, so this would have to do. "Let's do it."

* * * *

The living room was crowded. My mother stood next to David's John, who towered over her like a thin birch tree. She'd given up my father's church and was a practicing Catholic again. She loved the idea of us being married by a priest and begged John to dig out his old collar. He'd refused, and they'd compromised on a black suit jacket over a white turtleneck. She wore the same peach dress she had at the last wedding. My brother stood to one side talking with Tom and Jessica. They were the epitome of the American family, dressed in their Sunday best, with little Al in Jessica's arms.

They all looked up to watch David and me descend the stairs.

Kenny's old friend Nathan stood near the kitchen door, talking with Kenny's parents. Kenny's mother smiled warmly at me. Maybe she'd come to grips with the fact Kenny wasn't going to find a nice Jewish man and had decided an irreligious Polack wasn't so bad after all. Nathan looked solemn and professorial in his gray suit. Beside him floated Isaac, his incredibly young lover, so gorgeous he normally stopped traffic but today dressed to deflect attention, a sweet gesture from someone who knew how to steal a stage.

"He's here," Nathan called, looking toward the kitchen.

Kenny appeared and took my breath away. I was marrying the most gorgeous man in the room. He smiled his beautiful smile at me, and my nervousness melted. This was Kenny, who'd known me at my worst and loved me anyway. I reached for his hand.

Mom clapped her hands. "Al. Bring over that platter." She turned to John. "Father, would you bless the bread, wine, and salt?"

"Please, call me John, Mrs. Zajac. I'm not a priest anymore."

She waved her hand dismissively. "Of course you are. Once a priest, always a priest."

He smiled down at her. "I'm not sure the church would agree with you."

She looked at Kenny and me, standing before her holding hands. "I can't say I agree with the church about everything."

My brother held a silver tray on which sat a loaf of fresh baked bread and a saltshaker. Beside him, Jessica, who had handed her baby to his father, held a tray full of glasses in which rich red wine caught the light.

John turned to Kenny's father. "Would you like to do the blessing, sir?"

Kenny's dad smiled. He held up his glass and chanted in Hebrew. Kenny squeezed my hand. We might not have had a rabbi or a real priest, but we were all doing the best we could.

My mother took the loaf, tore off a chunk of bread, salted it, and held it out to us. "I didn't get to do this for your first wedding, George, and I think that was God's way of saying it wasn't right. May the two of you never be hungry, thirsty, or taste life's bitterness for as long as you live."

"Thank you, Mom." I had tears in my eyes as I took the bread from her, split it, and handed half to Kenny.

She nodded. "And if you want to give me grandchildren, I've been collecting information. It's not impossible."

Kenny choked on his bread.

"Really," she said. "There are surrogates, adoption—"

"Mom," Al stopped her. "Let's have the wine already."

"I'm just saying that I have information."

Kenny's mother stepped forward. "She's right. There are lots of resources. I can help too."

Jessica held out the tray of wineglasses. "Now you know what I lived with for the first couple years of my marriage. Drink up. Night feedings are just around the corner."

"Oh, no, they're not." Kenny downed half his glass. "I've had a hard enough time raising George—I'm not going through that again."

A horn honked outside. We all poured out onto the front lawn as a blue pickup came barreling into the driveway.

"Is that Pete?" Kenny asked. He turned to me. "Did you call him?"

Behind us Isaac cleared his throat. "I hope you don't mind. I was having a conversation with Avi—he and Pete are together now—and Avi said Pete knew you guys from Los Angeles and…"

David started laughing. "You think it's a big country, but it gets smaller and smaller all the time. How many degrees of separation?"

Pete jumped out of the truck and ran toward us. A handsome, dark-haired man followed him.

"It is so cool you guys are getting married." Pete threw one arm around me and another around Kenny and drew us into a group hug. He let us go. "I know I wasn't invited, but it's practically in my backyard and—"

Kenny slapped him on the back. "We're delighted you're here."

"We didn't come empty-handed." He turned to his companion. "This is Avi, by the way. Come on over to the truck. We brought homemade apple cider—leaded and unleaded—and my nephew's got us making cheese. We won an award last year. We brought enough food and drink even for a Polish wedding."

The afternoon sun shone on the green cornfields.

"Shall we get started?" John gestured toward the backyard, where folding chairs were set up in the footprint of the old barn.

Old ghosts sighed and died again as I stood next to Kenny, with David and Nathan on either side of us, rings in their pockets.

A hush fell behind us as John held up his hands. "Welcome. We are gathered here today to celebrate love, the great polisher of our tarnished souls."

I looked at Kenny. He smiled. My heart swelled. I considered myself an expert in weddings. But this one—with only a handful of guests, at the site of my nightmares, where even now the stench of cow shit tickled my memory—this wedding was better than anything I could imagine.

When it was time for the grooms to kiss, I pulled my husband into my arms and kissed him long and sweet in front of the ghost of my father, God, and the entire world.

Other Titles by Dev Bentham

About Dev Bentham

 Dev Bentham lives in Northern Wisconsin with her Boston terrier and Chicago sweetie. She has published short stories, poetry, newspaper articles and academic papers. She's worked in nearly every profession from waitress to professor to open-water diver and now writes gay romance out of an intense fascination with love, courage and gender.

Like most of us, her characters are flawed and damaged adults. They may not even know what they're looking for, but when they meet their bershert, their true love, their lives are transformed. Dev's stories are set in the real world where gay men have gay friends, families who do or don't accept them, personal histories they're not necessarily proud of and a myriad of experiences that have made them who they are.